"Forget Thor, it's Louie who really brings the thunder with this book. Action-packed, smart and very, very funny."

Rob Biddulph
author of
Draw With Rob

"A sheer doodle-filled comic delight."

DOMINIQUE VALENTE
author of Starfell

"THIS BOOK IS EXTREMELY FUNNY, HIGHLY ORIGINAL AND PACKED WITH QUIRKY DOODLES."

Nadia Shireen
author of Grimwood

"PUNCHY, FAST-PACED AND BLIMMIN' BRILLIANT."

Laura Ellen Anderson
author of Amelia Fang

"Laugh-out-loud funny, whip-smart observation, totally original & all round EPIC."

Hannah Gold
author of The Last Bear

"YOU **MUST** READ THIS BOOK, or may you get bitten on the bum by a snake, which could totally happen."

Jamie Smart
author of Bunny vs Monkey

"HILARIOUS, CLEVER, ADDICTIVE AND SO FULL OF HEART THAT I TRULY DIDN'T WANT IT TO END."

A. F. Steadman
author of Skandar and the Unicorn

"Loki is a hilarious and heartfelt read that promises an excellent and far from low-key series to come!"

L. D. LAPINSKI
author of
The Strangeworlds
Travel Agency

KT-447-275

This book belongs to:

LOKI

LOUIE STOWELL

LOKi

A BAD GOD'S GUIDE TO BEING GOOD

WALKER BOOKS

First published 2022 by Walker Books Ltd
87 Vauxhall Walk, London SE11 5HJ

4 6 8 10 9 7 5 3

Text and Illustrations © 2022 Louie Stowell

The right of Louie Stowell to be identified
as author of this work has been asserted in
accordance with the Copyright, Designs
and Patents Act 1988

This book has been typeset in Autumn Voyage, Avenir,
Bembo, Blackout, Cabazon, ITC American Typewriter,
Liquid Embrace, Neato Serif, OpenSans, Times and WB Loki.

Printed and bound by CPI Group (UK) Ltd, Croydon CR0 4YY

British Library Cataloguing in Publication Data:
a catalogue record for this book is available
from the British Library

ISBN 978-1-4063-9975-2
ISBN 978-1-5295-1054-6 (exclusive edition)

www.walker.co.uk

WALKER
BOOKS

FSC
www.fsc.org
MIX
Paper from
responsible sources
FSC® C171272

This book is dedicated to Adrian Mole, who ran so Loki could kind of stumble around messing everything up.

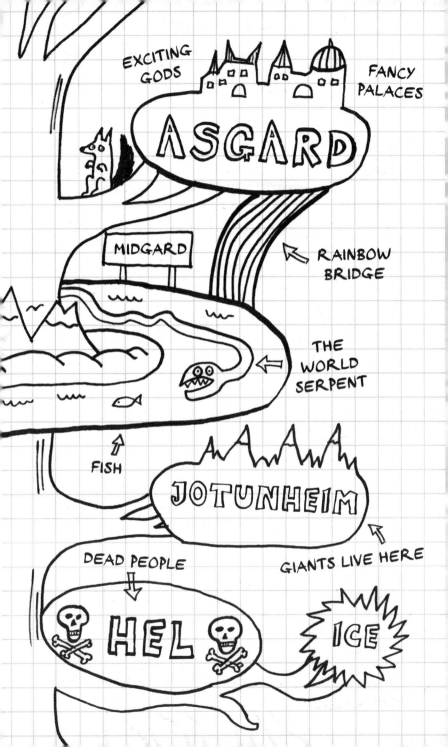

The Characters

LOKI

Me

VALERIE

THOR

HYRROKKIN

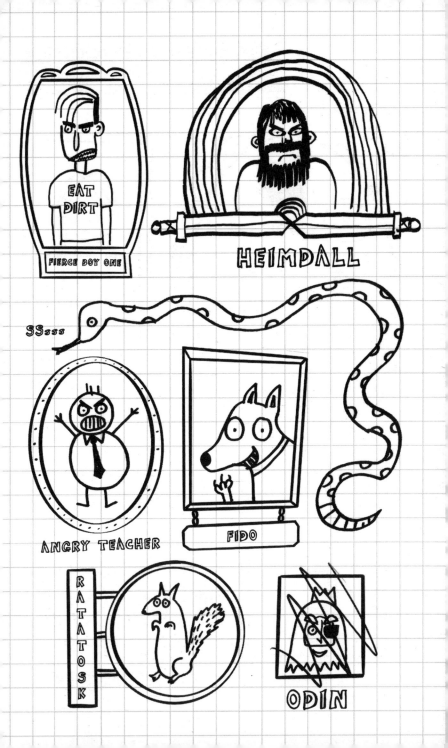

Timetable

		Monday	Tuesday
1		MATHS	MATHS
2		ART	HAND-WRITING
3		SPELLING	ENGLISH
4		TOPIC	GEOGRAPHY
5		PE	SCIENCE

BREAK

LUNCH

LOKI vs LUNCH BREAK

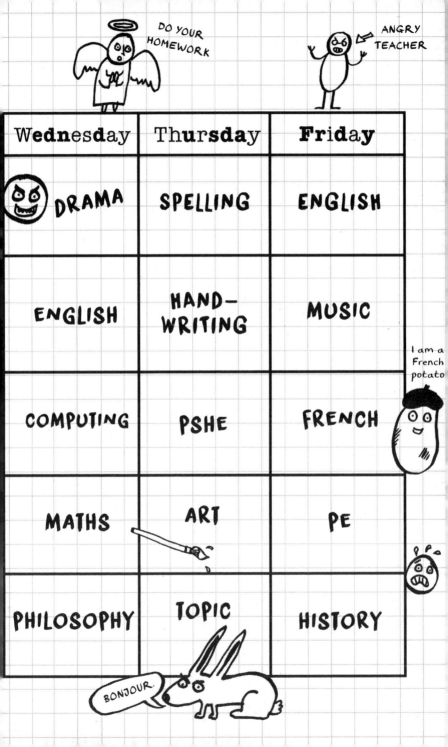

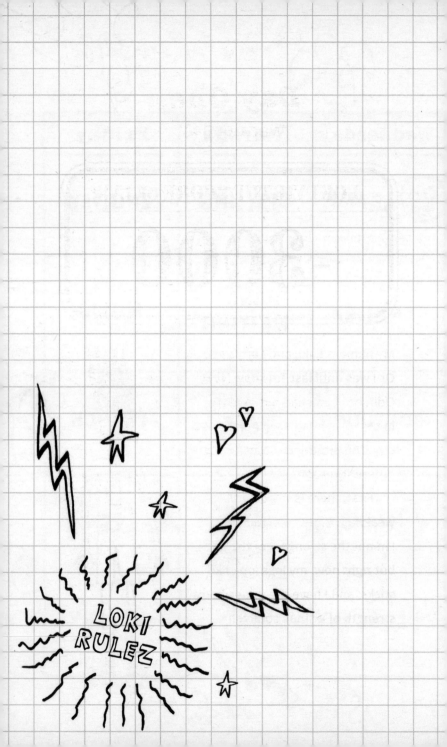

Day One:
Wednesday

LOKI VIRTUE SCORE OR LVS:

-3000

My name is Loki, and I am a god. Or I was until last Tuesday. Now, Odin has banished me to Earth in the form of an eleven-year-old boy. This situation is bad for many different reasons.

First, there is the overall weakness of this mortal body. I'm not the strongest of the gods, but right now, my legs look like sticks, and I have the upper-body strength of a small squirrel!

Turds.

15

Gods spring into being fully formed, so I have not, until now, ever been a child. Apparently, this is what Odin thinks I would look like as one! Rude!

BEFORE

AFTER

AWESOME BIG HAIR

HORNS

COOL FACIAL HAIR

BROAD SHOULDERS

ARM MUSCLES

ONLY SLIGHTLY AWESOME HAIR

SCRAWNY NECK

NOODLE ARMS

STICK LEGS

SHORT

Second, there are my fake parents. The guard god Heimdall (who hates me) and a terrifying giant called Hyrrokkin (feelings unknown) are here to pretend to be my father and mother while we are on Earth. I have to live with them and do what they say. I am appalled at this indignity. I'm thousands of years old! I should not have a bedtime! I should not have to do chores! I should absolutely under no circumstances be expected to fold my own undergarments!

Third, I must put up with eleven-year-old Thor, who seems to take great amusement from sitting on my head and farting. Perhaps I should take comfort in the fact that he is here and must suffer with me ... but it's hard to be comforted at the same time you're being farted on.

I am Thor, god of bum thunder!

While I am on Earth, I must write in this stupid book every single day for a month to prove that I'm becoming a better person and worthy of Asgard, whatever that means.

Now, you're probably thinking, "Loki, you are the god of lies, the greatest trickster of them all ... why don't you just lie in the book and say you've been very, very good all month?"

Sadly, Odin, in his annoying wisdom, has thought of that. This is a magical diary. If I lie in here, the diary will correct it. For example, if I say...

I AM THE MOST POWERFUL OF ALL THE GODS

! Correction: no, you are not. Odin is. You are a puny worm whose only real powers are physical transformation and being really sneaky.

... I get this kind of rude response.

So I have a choice: lie and be true to my glorious nature and be scolded by this random disembodied voice or tell the boring, unvarnished and usually unflattering truth.

> **Correction: I am not just any random voice. I am a simulation of Odin himself, with all his wisdom.** !

If you're so wise, what number am I thinking of?

> **You are not thinking of a number. You are thinking, "Odin smells".** !

Ah. In which case I may as well be honest in these pages. There's a first time for everything.

My tragedy began with a trick involving the goddess Sif, her long, golden locks, a pair of scissors and an ill-timed nap. I'll spare you the details, but let's just say that no one in Asgard can take a joke. Or a haircut.

The next thing I knew, I was clapped in chains, stripped of my divine powers and locked in a dungeon while Odin thought of a punishment.

Fast-forward to this morning, when I was rudely shoved out of my prison, blinking in the Asgardian sunshine. Odin thrust this book into my hands and booted me out from Asgard over the rainbow bridge down to Midgard – or, as you peasants call it, Earth.

As I fell, I transformed into my current puny shape. I landed down on Earth in a muddy puddle. Seconds later, Thor landed on top of me. Even as a human boy, he is not light. Plus he was clutching his favourite hammer, which made him even heavier. I now have some very purple bruises.

I picked myself up and looked around. I was in a sad grey place full of mortals. No one was looking at me. That's when I realized that my shape had been changed. Ordinarily, I am so beautiful to behold that all must look at me.

> **Correction: you are average-looking for a god, and the reason everyone stares at you in Asgard is because they're making sure you're not up to anything.** !

Have I mentioned I HATE the truth? It's so ugly and naked, like one of those mole rats that look like pink slug babies that have been chewing rocks.

↑ NAKED MOLE RAT

When Heimdall and Hyrrokkin arrived, they looked more or less like themselves, except Hyrrokkin was half her usual height, and Heimdall lacked his godlike glow.

Both were dressed in dowdy human clothing. Rather than animal pelts and many gold necklaces and bangles, Hyrrokkin's human attire made her look like she was about to attend a meeting for the Society of the Tedious and Humdrum. She was also on foot. Usually, she rides a wolf with snakes for reins.

Heimdall's bright armour and mighty weapons had been replaced by loungewear and slippers. They led me away to a hovel, where we were to live as a fake mortal family.

Correction: it is actually quite a nice house by human standards, with fast broadband and a power shower. All the above drawings are highly inaccurate if not technically lies.

Anyway, let us return to my horrifying new reality. In one of the small, sad rooms of our new dwelling, Heimdall and Hyrrokkin sat me down and gave me my orders.

> **!** **Correction: Hyrrokkin did not use her wolf to threaten you.**

The threat was implied. This whole thing is ridiculous. Heimdall and Hyrrokkin can't be trusted to report back to Odin on how much I've improved. They hate me.

Biased

Not objective

> **!** **Correction: Heimdall hates you, Hyrrokkin's on the fence. And they won't be reporting to Odin. That is for me, the diary, to measure.**

How about instead of rudely interrupting, you give me a pithy summary?

> **!** **Very well.**

- You, Loki, must show moral improvement as measured in virtue points. Your starting score is -3000. Your goal is +3000.

- The score will be measured by a book (me) containing all the wisdom of Odin himself, including important information about the twenty-first century.

- Hyrrokkin and Heimdall will supervise in the guise of parents.

- Thor, pretending to be your brother, will accompany you to places in the mortal realm where parents do not venture, such as school.

- You must not show your true godly powers to any human. Should you do so, you will be condemned to immediate and permanent punishment.

- Should humanity come to catastrophe during your time in Midgard, you will skip to immediate punishment.

Wait. I'm to blame for *anything* apocalyptically bad that happens when I'm on Earth? Even a meteorite strike? Or nuclear war? Or a plague of locusts?

> Plague? How rude!

> ! **Correct.**

UTTERLY UNFAIR!

> ! **In case of an emergency, you merely need to utter the words "HEY, ODIN" and the Allfather shall respond.**

I am too awesome to be treated like this! I am Loki, the cleverest, wittiest trickster! I refuse to spend a whole month doing only tedious, virtuous things. I shall no longer write in this diary! You're not the boss of me!

> HEY, ODIN! DO YOU HEAR ME? I'm not playing your game! I refuse! Come and get me!

It turns out Odin IS the boss of me and I will have to carry on recording my deeds in this diary, or else. Although it pains me to continue writing, here's what happened next...

"You refused your quest," said Odin. "This is the consequence. Meet Fangy, your new worst enemy."

"Let's not do anything hasty," I said, backing away from the snake's dripping venom. "We should talk about this like adults. Or like one adult and another adult in the body of a child."

Odin made a dismissive gesture, as though shooing away a naughty dog. "You're clearly too lazy to be good for even one month, so welcome to the rest of forever. A chamber where the air is thick with the smell of rotting fish and urine, with your least favourite song piped into your ears. Sif promises to come and cut your hair on a regular basis, leaving all those super annoying hairs you can never get rid of down your neck. And Thor will..."

"Please, oh Allfather, no," I begged. "I'll do anything. Please don't make me stay here." I shuddered. I didn't need to hear what further torture Thor's presence would entail.

Then there was the snake, weaving back and forth above me, dripping its sizzling poison.

Odin sniffed. "I don't believe you can do it. You're weak."

This stung. "I am NOT! I am Loki! I am a god! I can do ANYTHING!"

Odin looked at me for a long while in silence.

I held my breath – and not just because of the terrible smell.

"Your challenge stands. One month to prove you are worthy of Asgard. No more, no less. And if you fail…" He shook his head and gestured to the hissing serpent. I think it winked at me.

Then, without another word, I was back here in my ugly little chamber, lying on the uncomfortable bed, the tears drying on my face.

So it seems that Odin will read this diary at the end of the month and decide my fate. Will I return home, or will I be condemned to eternal torture?

DUN-DUN
DUNNNNNNN!
dramatic music

This is going to be a loooooooong month.

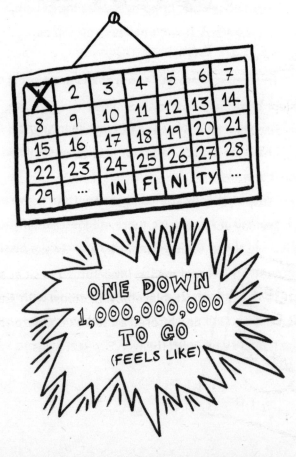

Day Two:
Thursday

What? How dare you!

I slept badly in the lumpy human bed. Where are my pillows of dove feathers and my eiderdown knit together with soft fluffy clouds? Say what you like about Asgard (and I often do) but its soft furnishings are second to none.

The day got no better. Instead of my usual breakfast of honey and ambrosia and roast meats, I was forced to sit at a tiny table, elbow to elbow with Thor, and offered a sad box emblazoned with the words WHEETY TREETS.

31

I came to understand that this was not a matter of bad spelling, but an attempt to be amusing.

Reader, the contents of the box were not treats, misspelled or otherwise. It was like eating grit coated in sugar. For some reason I cannot comprehend, they were drowned in milk until they went soggy, giving them the consistency of furry snot. Apparently many humans eat this every day? Not as part of a divine punishment, even.

It seems I have a lot to learn before I understand mortals.

To be fair, I have a lot to learn before I'll understand Thor. It baffles me that he's the one the gods admire. I once caught him cutting his toenails at the feasting table. I say "caught him" but actually, he cried out:

> Behold my mighty toenails! See how they sail across the feasting hall!

So I didn't have to do a great deal of detective work.

After our pathetic breakfast, Hyrrokkin walked us to the terrible place humans call school. Picture a prison full of cruel guards where the corridors smell of cleaning chemicals and despair, and you're about halfway to truly understanding the nature of mortal school.

We weren't allowed to travel by wolf because a) I'm not allowed to ride the wolf after last time and b) humans would run away in fear and that would lose me points.

33

Besides, Hyrrokkin has disguised her wolf as a dog. What self-respecting god would ride a DOG? But we did take it with us on our walk to school. Hyrrokkin said it would help us make friends. This seemed an absurd statement but, indeed, when we reached the school gates, a number of children clustered around us to stroke the dog.

Humans are so weird about dogs. They don't seem to realize that dogs are like wolves, but pathetic.

WOLF: AROOOOO!

1. Tears out throats

2. Howls at the moon in the dead of night

3. Looks cruel and awesome

DOG:

1. Never rips out throats

2. Sucks up to humans

3. Whines and makes annoying yappy sounds

4. Poos on the floor. Even THOR doesn't do that. Well, maybe once.

Hyrrokkin has renamed her wolf-in-dog-form Fido. Giants are known for many things – fighting, magic and trickery, building very big walls, shape-shifting – but imagination is definitely not one of their top qualities.

Once Hyrrokkin had turned around and walked the dog away, we joined a flood of mortal children flowing in through the school gates, all yelling and screaming and laughing.

We followed the throng into an empty outside area within the school walls – a sort of courtyard or, perhaps, a pen to contain these feral beings. They all yelled and fought and tussled like animals. Thor would no doubt fit right in here.

As we walked through this holding pen, which I later discovered was called the playground, many stopped to look at us. Or rather, at Thor.

It pains me to
say that all heads
turned to look at him.
Girls giggled as he passed.
Boys stood up a little straighter.
(Some giggled too.) Only one figure
didn't give him a glowing look of approval:
a tall, well-built girl with blonde plaits and a grim
expression. She glared at both of us as we passed. I
don't know if we'd done something to offend her, or
if that was just her face.

It was a familiar look for me. The same look
that had been on the goddess Sif's face after
she discovered I'd cut off her hair. In fact, it
was the look every god gave me at least
once a month, usually after I'd done
something witty and amusing.
I don't know *why* this girl
was giving me that look. I hadn't done
anything to her, other than walk past
being generally magnificent. Unless she
was jealous of my magnificence? It was
probably that.

We were greeted at the entrance to the school building by a woman wearing a loop of string around her neck upon which hung a terrible picture of that same woman. (Pointless.) The picture had her name beneath it. (Tedious.) She was, I discovered, what mortals call a teacher: an adult human who imprisons children during the day and yells facts at them. Like true villains, they set the children free each night to taste the joy of the outside world in order to make their recapture each morning a fresh torture.

"You must be Liam? And Thomas?" said the torturer. Odin had clearly given us fake names to better blend in among the mortals.

Yes, we are brothers. I'm the clever, handsome one.

Thor let out a growl, helpfully proving my point about my superior intellect.

37

"Er... OK. I'm Mrs Williams," said the teacher.

"Let me introduce you to the class."

Our "class" turned out to be a group of children all trapped together in a room, looking full of misery and woe.

Together with these other poor souls, we were given a series of challenges. Usually, the sort of trials that gods must undergo involve armed combat, or finding a magical object, or completing an impossible feat.

When you are a mortal child, these challenges mostly involve pens and paper.

For example, the first of our morning challenges involved writing simple words in a list to ensure we had used the correct runes – or letters, as the mortals call them these days.

Despite having machines called computers to help them write, mortals still appear to value words scratched out with simple implements. If I didn't scorn them all so much as worms beneath my notice, I'd find it rather charming and quaint.

I made some mistakes on purpose so no one would suspect I had the wit and wisdom of a god.

38

Thor made many mistakes because he has the wit and wisdom of a juvenile slug. Then we were given a break, because apparently puny mortal brains cannot absorb much knowledge at once.

After more tedious lessons it was time for lunch, which was inedible. No roast ox. No mead. Only soggy potatoes in grease and a green matter that I could not identify.

In one of the afternoon classes, we had to draw something called a family tree, which shows all your relations, from parents and children to brothers and sisters. Here is the example the teacher showed us.

It wasn't QUITE so straightforward for me, as I'm not entirely sure who my parents are, beyond the fact that my dad was probably a giant and my mum was

maybe a giant or a goddess, or possibly a bit of both.

Having unknown parents makes me much cooler, I think. Still, it might be nice to get the odd birthday card – or, in fact, know my actual birthday.

Here's what I drew:

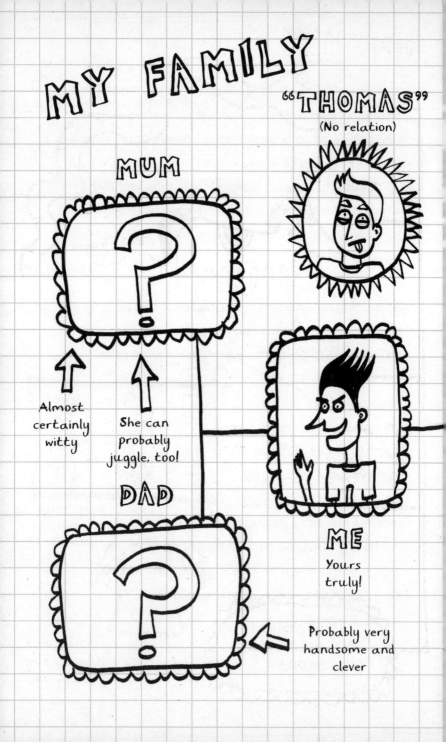

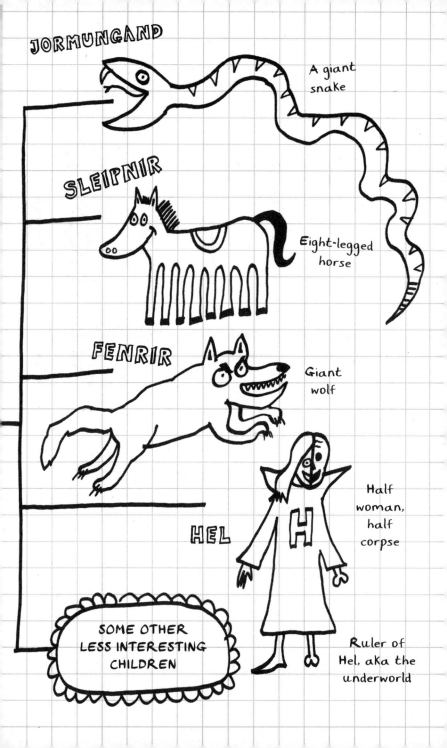

Instead of getting a standing ovation for my wonderful drawing skills and interesting, mysterious life, the teacher was furious.

The thing is, that snake IS my son! This book would say if that was a lie – and look... No lie!

(It's a long story, involving the strongest chain in the world, a wolf and a severed hand. I'll tell you sometime.) When I was allowed to return to my seat, Thor hissed at me.

Why did you draw your real family? We're not supposed to reveal our identities!

"No, we're not supposed to reveal our POWERS," I said. "That's what it says in the book."

"You know what Odin meant!" growled Thor. "You must keep the secrets of the gods!"

"It's not my fault if the instructions weren't clear."

"It's always your fault," growled Thor.

I hate Thor. I'll say one thing for the mortal realm: it opens up whole new avenues for disgusting tricks.

Thor's toothbrush

Whoosh

Day Three:

Friday

LOKI VIRTUE SCORE OR LVS:

-3100

50 points lost due to risking revealing his true nature, and the toilet toothbrush incident.

Huh. Well, that's not nice. I feel that this points system is deeply unfair. I would like to lodge a formal complaint.

! **Complaint noted. And ignored. The system was created by the Allfather, who knows all. You are a pain. Get on with your quest and stop whining.**

HUMPH. I had to walk the dog anyway, so I headed off with Thor, my pocket full of faeces bags. Mortal life is truly a long string of humiliations.

Heimdall, meanwhile, went off to something called a job. I didn't know what that was, but an explanation appeared in the book.

> **Job:** something human adults do. It means doing something you don't want to do, for people you despise, in exchange for gold.
>
> **(See also: CAPITALISM)**

Although Odin has supplied us with much gold to keep us clothed and fed while on Earth, Heimdall and Hyrrokkin agreed doing mortal jobs made it easier to fit in with the other humans and not attract too much attention.

Personally, I don't see why Odin couldn't have made us fantastically rich so no one would be surprised that Heimdall didn't work. Then we could have gone to expensive schools where they serve swan for every meal, instead of the slop I'm forced to eat. I've been reading up on private schools. I think I would enjoy attending one because there would be so many people worth making fun of.

Private School: a place where the children of the rich learn how to talk over each other and are told on a daily basis that they are born to rule the world. They inevitably grow up to be politicians and bosses and do indeed run the world, very badly.

But no, Odin only gave us enough gold to be comfortable, not enough to rule the world. Bah.

You shall not pass!

Heimdall is working as a security guard. This is a lot like what he did in Asgard, where he guarded the rainbow bridge to prevent attacking giants from coming in, only a security guard is not allowed to carry a huge axe and lop off the heads of anyone who tries to come into the building without permission. That would be actively frowned upon, in fact. Instead, Heimdall must ask to see a small square of plastic with their face on, then allow them inside. Humans appear to enjoy collecting and displaying these squares. And no wonder, for they wield great power.

Mystical human face square ⇨

NAME
A. Human

⇦ Talisman of great potency

Hyrrokkin is going to work as a dog walker – that means humans who have pet dogs pay her to walk their dogs. This feels very unfair. I'm walking our dog for free!

On the walk with Fido, Thor was twitchy. He kept looking from side to side.

"What's eating you?" I asked.

"We are in mortal bodies, not allowed to use our powers ... so I am preparing for a Frost Giant attack. It is inevitable they will come for us when we are at our weakest." He balled his hands into fists.

I need to be ready!

I sighed, deeply. Frost Giants are Thor's obsession. Well, giants in general, but particularly the icy variety. He doesn't mind Hyrrokkin, even though she is a giant, as she is a friend of the gods who has proven her loyalty time and again. Which, now I think about it, makes me like her considerably less.

Of course, when we gods talk about giants, we don't mean people big enough to uproot trees or buildings. Giants often aren't even that big. That might be a lot for your tiny mortal mind to grasp, but it's true.

Hyrrokkin, for example, in her proper form is larger than most gods, but she still doesn't need to duck to walk through the palace doors in Asgard.

Plus, giants are shape-shifters, so they don't even look humanoid half the time. Hyrrokkin is very fond of turning into a swan and going for a paddle.

Giant

Also a giant

This one too

Yup, even this duck

I should know about the shape-shifting. I'm (at least) part giant, so I can shape-shift brilliantly. Although, sadly, I'm not as strong as a giant.

No one officially knows exactly how the gods-versus-giants feud started, except for Odin. I believe it had something to do with him slaying the very first giant and using its body to create the Earth. Not that Odin would ever admit that.

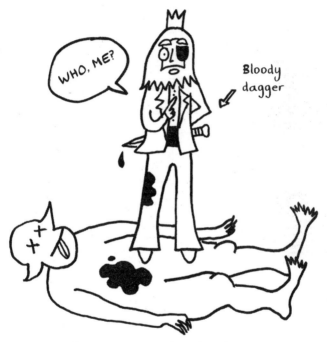

So we all go along with the idea that it's a great mystery why the giants hate us so much.

Personally, I like the giants-versus-gods thing. Bitter feuds keep eternity interesting!

But Thor HATES giants. Especially Frost Giants, who are the toughest, most powerful and – perhaps this goes without saying – most icy of the giants. They're not exactly made of ice, but there's always a hint of frost around their faces, and getting punched by one is like being slammed into by an iceberg.

I hadn't thought of the Frost Giants since we'd arrived on Earth really. I'd been too busy gnashing my teeth over my cruel fate. Now that Thor mentioned it, it was a little worrying that we were so weak and defenceless in these mortal forms. As this body bruises easily, I shall try to avoid violence at all costs.

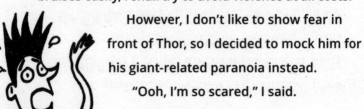

However, I don't like to show fear in front of Thor, so I decided to mock him for his giant-related paranoia instead.

"Ooh, I'm so scared," I said.

We didn't speak for the rest of the walk.

He did, however, punch me very hard in the arm.

Then, to add insult to arm injury, it was time for school. The school day went something like this:

ASSEMBLY – sitting on a cold, uncomfortable floor being talked at by very boring teachers. I didn't listen, so I couldn't tell you what they said.

ENGLISH – We had to read a poem and explain what it meant. I pointed out to the teacher that it was meaningless drivel. Poems should be about wars or epic hand-to-hand combat or – my personal favourite genre – insults about your mortal enemies. This poem was just about some daffodils and clouds and the poet's feelings. Nothing exciting happened at all! The teacher made me sit in the corner to think about my behaviour, which only goes to show that mortals cannot accept literary criticism.

BREAK – We were herded outside into the depressing grey concrete pen of the playground and expected to enjoy ourselves. Thor quickly started to play a ball game with some of the boys, while I stood on the sidelines, tactically observing, and definitely not being left out and ignored.

! You and I both know that's a lie, Loki...

MUSIC – For one accustomed to the glorious melodies of Asgard, this was a brutal awakening. If you have never heard instruments called glockenspiels played by a class of talentless mortal children, count yourself a fortunate soul.

FRENCH – a mortal language, apparently only used to discuss holidays, food and train tickets. Useless to me anyway, given that I have the ability to understand all languages on Earth without even thinking about it.

After lunch, which was every bit as disgusting as the day before, we had an hour of ritual pain and humiliation. The official name for it was "physical education" but I knew the truth. The teacher was clearly a sadist who wanted us all to experience weakness and shame. Mortal bodies, I discovered, give off a smelly, salty liquid when they overheat. Revolting. Loki does NOT sweat.

But apparently "Liam" does. The shame! The dampness! The stench!

Meanwhile, Thor – aka Thomas – showed off. Everyone fawned on him like the puny mortal peasants they are.

HISTORY – actually quite interesting. It mostly covered things that happened since the last time I was on Earth, which was about 1,000 years ago, give or take a century. Apparently mortals like fighting wars a LOT – and invading and stealing each other's stuff while pretending it's for their own good. This is something called colonialism and it's twisted even for a trickster like me! And, get this, there are special crime scenes that you can visit full of the stolen stuff. They're called museums. I must ask my fake parents to take me to one because, honestly, it sounds made up that anyone would flaunt their theft like that. When I steal things, at least I'm sneaky about it!

Finally, after roughly nine million years had passed, it was time to go home. Thor and I walked out of the gates. I caught sight of that girl with plaits out of the corner of my eye. I stopped to watch as two large boys came over to her. They had a fierce look – like Thor did the time I hid his hammer.

56

She was biting her lip and it was wobbling like a flimsy chair under Thor's bulk.

While I tend to enjoy cruelty, I felt a bit disappointed in these boys. Their put-downs were neither clever nor funny. While I tutted at their lack of imagination, Thor strode over.

Subterfuge is not his finest skill.

Thor bunched his very large fists and stepped forward. He loomed. He isn't even that tall, but he has a way of looming over people, even people taller than him. It was like he cast a bigger shadow than most mortals. There was a faint crackle of lightning around him. Apparently HIM nearly revealing his godly powers wasn't against the rules. Such a daddy's boy.

Fierce Boy One stepped back. Fierce Boy Two stepped behind him.

Whatever. Let's go. I'm bored.

He was not bored. He was about to wet his pants with fear. Having made a mortal do that in the past, I know all the signs – and smells.

As the two boys scuttled away, Thor came back towards me. Valerie walked over, looking embarrassed. I prepared myself. She was going to give Thor The Look, wasn't she? Halfway between the eyes of a cow and a puppy. They always put on a Voice too. Like honey and sadness.

Except Valerie didn't. She tilted her head and seemed to weigh him up.

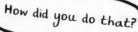

How did you do that?

Her voice was more suspicion than honey.

"What?" said Thor.

"Make them go away?"

"I am clearly very strong and muscular and they were scared," said Thor.

58

He didn't usually have to explain himself. He was the mighty Thor! All trembled at his fists! Or got punched across the room.

But no one knew he was Thor, or that he was mighty.

Hmm. Thanks, anyway, but I don't need defending.

One thing about this whole situation fascinated me.

"Why didn't you insult them back?" I said.

"I didn't want to give them the satisfaction of sinking to their level," said Valerie, folding her arms. "My mothers say that's the best way to react to bullies. Eventually they'll get bored. I'd prefer to go riding and forget about them."

Thor wrinkled his nose. "But surely the best way to react to bullies is to hit them with a m—"

"Hit them with a medley of creative insults," I finished, elbowing him in the stomach before he could say "magical hammer". Honestly, that immortal oaf is a liability.

OOOF

Valerie shook her head. "No, that's not it."

She still looked suspicious, so I thought I should reinforce our mortal cover.

"I'm Liam Smith and this is my far inferior twin brother, Thomas. Obviously I got the looks AND the brains."

"I'm Valerie Kerry," said Valerie. "And my mothers are waiting for me, so I have to go."

Valerie hurried away, casting one last suspicious look at us both.

What an odd mortal.

I could tell he was annoyed she didn't give him The Look. I grinned.

I like her.

As we left the school, a cat came over and rubbed up against my legs. I like cats. Unlike dogs, they're not sycophantic. They only give you affection if they choose to. Obviously it chose to give me affection because I am glorious. Also, this particular cat was the perfect opportunity to mock Thor for his jumpiness this morning.

"OH NO!"

"Help!" I said to Thor. "I'm being attacked by a Frost Giant."

"Shut up," growled Thor. "You shouldn't joke about serious things."

"I'm very serious," I said as the cat pushed its face into my hand, requesting to be stroked. "It's purring me to death. It's brutalizing me with its soft fur! I die! See how it devours me!" I added as the creature licked my hand, purring louder.

PRRRR

Thor turned and stalked towards the school gates with a snort. I stayed to stroke the school cat for a minute. It seemed to really like me! I mean, of course it did. I am marvellous and wonderful. It's just a shame that only this cat seems to realize that fact.

I love Loki.

Thor smells of bums.

He's the best god.

Day Four:
Saturday

Today is a Saturday, which in the mortal realm means no school. This should be a time of great rejoicing and pleasure, but Hyrrokkin decreed that we should go for a "nice healthy walk". This was because she could "feel my mortal form withering" and "my death approaching hour by hour" but also because "if I am cooped up in the house for one minute longer with Loki I may kill him with my bare hands".

She made me get out of bed as the sun rose and instructed me to put on several pairs of socks, which I refused to do! I am Loki! I wear what I like!

After another sad mortal breakfast, we all climbed into a strange carriage that burned poisonous fumes in order to move forward.

Car: a mortal vehicle that is the perfect example of their inability to see the bigger picture. Cars burn poisonous fumes to move forward, which fills the air with a foul stench and slowly kills the planet. And yet humans like them because they "look cool" and go "vroom vroom vroom".

Hyrrokkin directed the vehicle using some kind of witchcraft that she focused through a wheel-shaped talisman. We navigated through crowded streets full of similar vehicles until we reached the edge of town. Thor and I had to sit in the back, strapped in our chairs with Fido drooling on my shoulder as Heimdall made us listen to something called a playlist, which turned out to be series of songs chosen by him. Now, some of the gods have very good taste in music. In fact, we even have a god OF music. But Heimdall is definitely NOT it.

PLAYING: "NOW THAT'S WHAT I CALL PAST IT" by We Used to Be Cool

By the time we reached our destination, my ears wanted to run away and hide.

The walk itself was a forced march through muddy fields, with Hyrrokkin barking directions and Heimdall disagreeing with those directions as they tried to read a mortal map. Apparently this is a traditional ritual among mortal couples, and Heimdall explained that it was important to seem like normal humans. But there was no one there to witness the display, so I'm not sure they had to commit to their roles QUITE so shoutily.

That is CLEARLY east!!!

You say this to one who has navigated the vast icy wastes of Jotunheim and lived, FOOL!

Map

compass

Thor enjoyed himself thoroughly, ignoring their bickering, stopping to play in the mud and climb trees and generally show off his physical prowess to the surrounding cows and rabbits. I swear they gave him The Look. Even rabbits! Even cows!

Meanwhile, I had wet feet and my fake parents were arguing and I contemplated killing them all. But then how would I get home? I didn't know how to command the magical vehicle.

Also, killing my fake family would – just guessing – lose me points.

A wise guess. !

Eventually, many hours later, we returned to the vehicle. Although we were still alive, no one was talking and I had horrifying pustules on my feet, which are apparently a mortal affliction called blisters. None of the others had blisters because they wore two pairs of socks under their shoes. I have regrets.

When we got home, I saw that Valerie girl lurking near our house. I think she's spying on us. I take back my earlier liking of her! I smell trouble ... and a slight hint of horse. I don't like it. (The trouble, I mean. Horses are fine by me. In fact, I *was* a horse once. A mare, if you want to be technical about it. Long story involving a very dodgy builder and me nearly losing the sun, the moon and the goddess Freyja. Remind me to tell you about it when I'm not being spied on.) I fear that if Valerie observes me too closely, she might guess my true godly nature – which is surely evident to anyone who watches my magnificence for long enough – and I'll lose the quest! Then it will be Snakesville for me, population one! Two, counting the snake.

Day Five:
Sunday

LOKI VIRTUE SCORE OR LVS:

-3100

I'll give you a pass for planning to kill your family because you took it back quickly.

Valerie was lurking again when Thor and I went to an empty wasteland known as the park. She was sitting on a moving chair known as a swing and appeared to be taking notes as she watched me. I definitely did not like it.

I wonder if I can plot Valerie's death safely? I thought.

"Hey, Odin," I said, using the command I'd been instructed to use to attract attention from the Allfather. I said it too quietly for anyone nearby to hear, but Odin hears everything, even when you call him a

bad name, such as poo-breath or stinkface, under your breath.

"Hey, Odin!" I muttered. "What do you say? Can I plot a mortal's death if they deserve it for spying on me and still not lose points? After all, as well as stopping her from blabbing my secrets to the world, I'd be able to show a LOT of moral improvement if I started out by killing someone – the only way would be up! Two birds with one stone!"

As I said this, a squirrel scuttled over to me. Thor was surrounded by admirers, who were very impressed with his ability to move a ball around using his feet. But I stood all alone, in a lofty solitude that was clearly my own choice and not because no one wanted to spend their leisure time with me.

> **!** I think even YOU know you're lying there, Loki.

Stop interrupting, that's very rude!

> **!** I'm just doing my job.

Fine! Anyway, what was I saying? Oh yes, so, the squirrel hopped onto the top of a bench and looked me in the eye.

I spotted Valerie Kerry watching me across the park as I spoke to the squirrel. I realized it might look strange to her, so I conjured an acorn in my pocket and fed it to Ratatosk, who ate it greedily, then scampered away, presumably back to Odin.

So ... I won't kill her. But I'll have to be careful around her.

Day Six:
Monday

LOKI VIRTUE SCORE OR LVS:

-3150

50 points lost due to plotting the death of a mortal.

I can't believe my score keeps going down! I didn't even plot her death! I just thought about maybe plotting it!

! If you don't like this quest, you're welcome to start your eternity of snake venom right now. Also, you had your warning. Plotting deaths = bad, whether the proposed victims are mortals or gods.

OK, OK! I'll accept the scoring system. But I don't have to like it.

Speaking of scores, we had something called a test at school today. I didn't know the answers, and the teacher did not applaud my creativity in making them up.

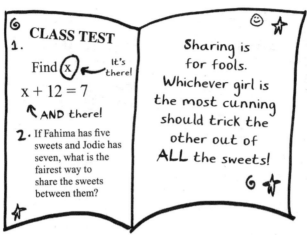

CLASS TEST

1. Find x — It's there!

$x + 12 = 7$

AND there!

2. If Fahima has five sweets and Jodie has seven, what is the fairest way to share the sweets between them?

Sharing is for fools. Whichever girl is the most cunning should trick the other out of ALL the sweets!

In Art class, I drew a picture of the teacher. This made him angry, which was very silly of him. If an Art lesson is not meant to inspire children to create art, then what is the point of it?

There were other lessons. Let us not speak of them, for their tedium would decay my soul to recount. I feel grey and weak even thinking about the twenty minutes I had to spend on a cruel torture called fronted adverbials. It involved learning entirely made-up rules about word order, for a language that probably won't exist by the next time I visit Earth in another thousand years!

To end the day (and make me long for the end times) we had physical education. Thor was showing off shamelessly. Without technically revealing his powers, he performed feats that were way beyond the average ability of a human child.

Everyone was giving him The Look. I wanted to barf.

Knowing my luck, if I did puke all over Thor, Odin would probably take off points.

When the teacher asked if Thor had been approached by any professional sports teams for their youth leagues, I let out a sound of pure disgust. I couldn't let this lie. I had to stop everyone from fawning over him. I excused myself to go to the toilet, then used my powers *in private* to transform into that creature most beloved of foolish humans: a dog.

BLEURGH!

That dog – that totally ordinary dog, definitely not a god revealing his powers to humanity, but a loyal hound of Earth, with a waggy tail and a slobbery tongue – then ran onto the sports field, streaking past Thor and attracting the attention of all the children. Thor's stardom was no more. It was all about the dog.

Soon, everyone was chasing me... I mean the dog shouting about where it, the dog, not me, might have come from. The dog left a small gift on the ground for Thor to step in. Annoyingly, he jumped over it. But the teacher didn't. The teacher skidded in the poo and fell on his bottom with a jarring thump and a yelp of pain.

Something called an ambulance came not long after. I managed to hide in a bush and transform.

"What happened?" I asked in an innocent voice. "I had to go to the toilet."

"A teacher slipped on a dog poo!" said a small, skinny boy. "It was the best thing I have ever seen!"

"Did he now?" I asked even more innocently.

I felt powerful fingers gripping my neck. Thick, Thor-y fingers.

"You aren't supposed to use your powers," he hissed, dragging me away from the action. The teacher was being stretchered into the ambulance and I had wanted to get a better view of the glorious chaos.

I took a moment to bathe in the joy of a job well done.

I had to stop bathing when our class was called into the school hall to be shouted at for "letting a dangerous dog onto the premises". Unless someone confessed, the whole school would have detention!

I didn't keep quiet out of cowardice. It's just that I DIDN'T let a dog onto the premises. I was the dog. Ergo I'm not guilty.

Hmm...   !

The detention was very tedious. Sitting still for an hour is not what I was made for, so I kept myself occupied by whispering insults at Thor.

As we were leaving after detention, the school cat came up and brushed against my ankles. It started purring. I was surprised, given how recently I'd been a dog, but perhaps the smell had worn off by then.

"I hate cats," growled Thor.

"But your auntie Freyja drives a chariot pulled by them!" I pointed out. "She gives you lifts in it all the time!"

"Yes, and they smell," said Thor gloomily. "But I miss home. Even the smelly cats. This is all your fault."

"You can't blame the cats being smelly on me," I said. "I'm not the one who feeds them pickled herring."

"You know that's not what I meant," said Thor. "Why do you have to always twist my words?"

"Loki gonna Loke," I said.

"Loki gonna be punished for all eternity with snake venom, more like," said Thor. He began to cheer up after that.

That afternoon, when I returned to my achingly dull human abode, Heimdall and Hyrrokkin were waiting for me.

As soon as I came through the door, Hyrrokkin held out a hand.

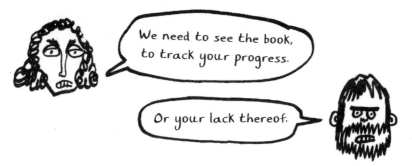

We need to see the book, to track your progress.

Or your lack thereof.

Heimdall hates me just a little bit more than the other gods do, even though he has rarely been on the receiving end of my tricks. I think it's because he completely lacks a sense of humour.

> **Correction:** It's because Heimdall believes in order and justice and you are an agent of chaos and destruction. Also the last time you tricked him, you lost his pet hamster, Mr Tibbles.

This diary is such a drag. Facts get in the way of a good story so often, don't you think? I like my version better where it's about him being an unfunny killjoy and I am not at fault.

Hyrrokkin took the book off me and leafed through it, frowning. Then she passed it to Heimdall.

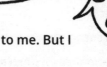

Aha! It is as I suspected. You are FAILING!

Obviously this wasn't news to me. But I didn't like having it rubbed in.

"I suggest you start performing some virtuous acts," said Hyrrokkin. "And make it quick."

"Or, subject yourself to an eternity of snakes," sniffed Heimdall. "You deserve it after what you did to Mr Tibbles!"

Hyrrokkin sighed. "Heimdall, Odin gave us the task of helping Loki on his quest. You could at least pretend to obey him. No skin off my nose, you understand; he's not MY king, but maybe you should try a bit harder to *help* Loki?"

"Yeah, I thought you LIKED taking orders from the big boss man," I said.

"Silence!" growled Heimdall. But then he sighed and said, "I suppose I could give you a few helpful hints. If you want to improve your score, try doing something nice for someone. Something helpful. Something that doesn't directly benefit you but helps someone else."

I saluted as sarcastically as I could. "Yes! Sir!"

Heimdall scowled. "Go away and think of how to be better."

I went to my room and wrote in this book and drew a portrait of Heimdall.

Ssssoon...

Day Seven:
Tuesday

LOKI VIRTUE SCORE OR LVS:

-3250

100 points lost due to hospitalizing a teacher and spreading suffering across the whole school via detention.

OK, I'm going to get serious about this whole "being good" thing. I am not a coward, but I will freely admit that eternal damnation and snake venom scare me.

! **Correction: you are a coward. You have run away from dozens of battles screaming, "Please don't hit me. Not the face!"**

Fine, whatever. However, it's not just about the snakes and the torture part. I can't stay any longer in this sad little place. I have to get back to Asgard!

Life wasn't perfect there, but it was so GRAND! Everything here is small and insignificant.

Rubbish

I miss the feasts in Asgard. I miss the dancing. I miss the beautiful gardens and the luxurious clothes. I had this one robe that was so soft it was like being snuggled by a pile of puppies. I even miss the people. Sure, they didn't trust me and, one time, they sewed up my mouth as a punishment. But I was working on them! They were going to learn to love me any moment! I just needed more time!

SO TOASTY.

Hmmm... dubious.   !

Shut up, diary. So, anyway, I need to get my score up so I can get out of here and back up there. I've discovered that humans find out information about how to do things using the internet.

An At-A-Glance Guide To Mortal Life In The 21st Century

Internet, the: Picture the internet like the severed head of the wise god Mimir that Odin keeps in his palace to dispense advice, only with no will of its own, and as though Mimir had taken to randomly spouting nonsense and lies. The internet is a web of invisible roots, like those of the World Tree that connects all nine realms. It allows humans to be cruel to each other from a distance, to watch moving pictures of animals and to play games of great violence with one another. (See also: GAMES, VIDEO.)

I decided to try using the internet to help me after breakfast this morning. Heimdall has a computer that he uses to do research into mortal customs and lets me use it when he doesn't need it.

! **Correction:** you sneak on to it when he's not looking.

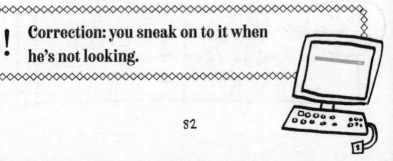

That's his fault for not understanding the concept of passwords. So, I began my research...

HOW TO BE A GOOD PERSON   Search

One of the first things that the computer spat back was "listen to your own conscience, that voice inside you telling you what's right".

I don't think I have a conscience. When I listen for a voice inside me telling me what's right, all I hear is...

I decided I might be better off asking people who are already considered "good".

First, I went to see Thor. He was busy arranging his hammer collection. His favourite hammer, Mjolnir, was in pride of place.

Anyway, I asked him what he thought being a good person meant.

Then I asked Heimdall and Hyrrokkin:

Be humble.

Be honest. If you're capable of it.

At school, I asked the teachers:

Help people.

Let others go first.

With all this in mind, I wrote a list of things to try:

Be brave
Be humble
Be honest
Be helpful
Let others go first

I tried out being honest first. Although I enjoy lying, it turns out that I'm actually very good at telling the truth.

Then I walked away, glowing with pride from a job well done. I could hear him howling at me as I walked away, no doubt praising my name and my virtue.

In Maths class, I tried letting others go first. The teacher asked who would like to come up to the front and write the answers to some hard sums on the board. I put my hand up. "Jamal would like to go first," I said, pointing at a very nervous-looking boy. "He's really keen and I am happy to wait! I'm a good person like that."

Next, I moved on to being helpful.

I started with one of my classmates, a girl called Laura, who had handwriting worthy of a four-year-old writing in mud with a stick. I pointed this out to her, in case she hadn't noticed, giving her the chance to improve, which I think was very helpful!

She started crying and had to leave the room.

I considered that I may need to practise being helpful before I fully cracked it. But I am a god! I can do anything!

Later, I gave the teacher some helpful feedback in our Science lesson.

She didn't cry, so I think I'm making progress. Of course, she did excuse herself to go to the toilet for a very long time, leaving us with the teacher's assistant, but she probably needed to do a poo.

At the end of the day, I had another go at being kind and helpful. There's a girl in my class who still sucks her thumb, so at the school gates I went to see her parents.

"I wanted to tell you that you're failing as parents," I said in my sweetest, kindest voice. "Your daughter shouldn't still be sucking her thumb. I think perhaps you don't love her enough, or perhaps you love her TOO much, and she's not able to grow up because you pander to her too much? Anyway, hope that helps!"

The parents stared at me as I skipped off down the road, feeling like that went rather well. No tears!

Day Eight:
Wednesday

LOKI VIRTUE SCORE OR LVS:

-3300

50 points lost due to cruelty to teachers,
pupils and parents.

! Note: over the previous day, Asgard witnessed an
uptick in prayers from the general area of Loki's
school. Many of these prayers were for the new
boy to have an unfortunate accident. This does
not reflect well on Loki's progress.

GAH. I tried to be good in so many ways, and none of
them worked. What does Odin WANT from me???

Anyway. Enough about what Odin wants. I know
what I want: a smartphone.

An At-A-Glance Guide To Mortal Life In The 21st Century

Smartphone: a handheld device containing the sum of human knowledge. It connects to the internet, a place of both rage and mirth, and of many lies. (See also: INTERNET, THE.)

I've noticed the teachers giving them out at the end of the day. When I tried joining the cluster of children around the teacher's desk to take one for myself, I was accused of stealing. Me, Loki! Outrageous. I am a trickster not a thief. Well ... not today.

Before school, I asked Heimdall and Hyrrokkin if I could have a smartphone. They said no.

We suspect you only want it to play tricks.

Why should we trust you with one?

"Ah," I said. "But can you trust me WITHOUT one? If you give me a smartphone, you can contact me at any time. And, after all, what harm can I do with a simple communication device? It is merely a tool that allows you to transmit messages over distances – like a raven, but it doesn't poo."

Heimdall said he wouldn't trust me with a raven either, after the time I put glue on Odin's shoulders so the ravens got stuck when they landed to whisper in his ears.

Instead, Heimdall has decided that he can help me become a better person by reading parenting books. He spread them all over the breakfast table so there was hardly room for me to wedge myself in and eat my pathetic bowl of brown sludge.

GLUE

WHEN BOYS GO BAD

A Parent's Guide to Bad Behaviour

HOW TO RAISE A SON WHO IS NOT A CRIMINAL MASTERMIND

Parenting for People Who Don't Want Their Kids to End Up in Prison

BEAT THEM WITH STICKS, IT'S GOOD FOR THEM

(Those were not the exact titles, but who has the spare mental energy to remember book titles when you're staring down the barrel of an eternity of snake torture?)

"Since you are in the form of a mortal boy, perhaps I can shape and guide you like one," Heimdall explained as he took a spoonful of WHEETY TREETS.

"We should also play some sports as a family," said Hyrrokkin. "It is supposed to bond humans together, and exercise will slow the inevitable decay of these fragile mortal bodies. I quite fancy boxing. It looks duly violent."

"Is that the one where the ball is shaped like an egg and the rules are more complex than the mystical proclamations of the Norns, who rule all our fates?" asked Heimdall.

"No, it's the one where people punch one another in the face and elsewhere on the body," said Hyrrokkin.

Personally, I think punching these fragile mortal bodies would accelerate the decay.

I took this opportunity to slink away and get ready for school before they forced me to play any of these terrifying human sports.

Today at school we had a lesson called Drama.
This, to my delight, involved pretending to
be other people. This is something I am an
expert at, as a shape-shifter with a love of
lies and deception.

IT ME!

Actually, it was a pretty good day at school, all
in all. Later on we had Computing, which was most
excellent. I was supposed to be using the computer
to program variables. But that sounded tedious, so
instead, I used the internet to discover new rude
words in mortal languages.

Turns out the word for bum is a variable!

Les fesses

Sadly, my good mood did not continue. After
school, I asked Hyrrokkin and Heimdall for a phone
again, so I could use the internet whenever I wanted.

They said no. I sulked in my room. Sulking is a power that I understand mortal children wield over their parents.

Unfortunately, Heimdall's parenting book covers sulking, so he was not fooled and left me to it. So here I lie on my bed sighing, feeling lonely and sad and – from what I can hear from the loud lip-smacking noises Thor is making downstairs – missing out on foodstuffs.

Day Nine:
Thursday

LOKI VIRTUE SCORE OR LVS:

-3300

Holding steady.

Ah, how can it be that I, who have known immortality, living through aeons, can find one single mortal day so long? That's school for you.

As part of my mission to obtain a smartphone, when school FINALLY finished I slipped away from Thor and hid in the park near our home until it was past dark. I was shivering with cold and hunger, but sometimes you must suffer for your cause.

Who knew being righteous would be so chilly?

By the time I staggered home, Heimdall and Hyrrokkin were on the verge of summoning Odin to help find me, and Thor had come very close to beating up a man he saw outside our home because he suspected he was a Frost Giant who'd kidnapped me. Even Fido gave me a lick to welcome me home.

I was actually a little bit touched, until they all started shouting at me – and then Heimdall made me listen to an hour-long lecture about personal responsibility. It had charts and diagrams. Is it possible to die of boredom? I fear I may find out if that happens again...

Day Ten:
Friday

LOKI VIRTUE SCORE OR LVS:

-3350

50 points lost for running off and making Heimdall and Hyrrokkin worry and risking Thor visiting physical violence upon an innocent mortal.

Today in History we learned about the Roman Empire, which was highly unnecessary for me and Thor, because we are old enough that we were still regularly visiting the mortal realm back then.

GRRR

Well, perhaps it was necessary for Thor, given that he asked the teacher if the Roman Empire was the one where they built the pyramids, which as any immortal – or, indeed, most eleven-year-old mortal children – can tell you was the ancient Egyptians.

The teacher got very excited about my superior knowledge regarding Romans and asked if I'd studied it in my old school. I lied beautifully and told her that yes, I had read many books about it. She asked me to talk about my favourite part of Roman life, then got very quiet when I started describing the gladiatorial games in great detail. Just as I was getting going, describing how a lion ate someone alive and the crowd went wild as it spat out his bloody foot, the teacher told me to please stop, as some of the children were looking very upset.

(I said that in my head, because I was starting to get a feeling that if I said any more out loud she might eat me like that lion did the gladiator.)

When I got home from school, a phone was waiting for me. Totally worth losing points for! It was even worth the lecture!

"Don't take this as licence to run off again. But I suppose we SHOULD have a way of contacting you when inevitably you go rogue," grumbled Heimdall.

"Very responsible parenting," I said with a serious expression. Then I grabbed the phone and ran upstairs to play with it. (Figuring out how to do this took several hours. Technology has definitely become more complicated in the last thousand years.)

I had a thoroughly enjoyable couple of hours with my smartphone, including changing the ringtone to Odin's voice saying "FARTS". But then I tired of it. How can mortals spend all their lives attached to such items?

Hmm, maybe I will watch ONE more video of a raccoon acting like a person...

Day Eleven:
Saturday

LOKI VIRTUE SCORE OR LVS:

-3400

For taking the voice of Odin in vain
and making it say "FARTS".

No, you're a fart.

In the end, I did not go to bed until two in the morning. It turned out there were many, many more videos of raccoons on the internet that required I watch them.

But, joy of joy, Saturdays mean no school. And, after the obligatory Fido walk, there would be nothing between me and doing whatever I desired.

I started out doing some more exploring of the internet on my phone. I insulted some people and spread a few lies. It only seemed polite to do so, as that's what other mortals use it for, and who am I to tell them their customs are worthless?

MESSENGER

Loki: Coal is edible.

Loki: You smell

Loki: Climate change is fake

Next, I decided to participate in another human custom: shopping.

Shopping: a habit that can involve exchanging gold for goods but often means merely walking agonizingly slowly around a place with buildings called shops, looking at things you can't afford and not buying them.

I don't see the appeal but, like I said, I'm humbly bowing to human customs. So, I walked into town with Thor, who came to stop me "thieving, pillaging or otherwise creating chaos". We came to a row of glass-fronted buildings that I realized must be the places they call shops.

I'd never been in a shop before. The last time I came down to Earth, humans sold things to one another in open-air markets. I have very fond memories of watching a dancing bear that I then set loose. But these sad little shops had no animals, dancing or otherwise.

It was then that I saw something out of the corner of my eye. Further down the road, my suspicions were confirmed!

Valerie was following us!

Thor did not care. "She's probably out shopping. Like us. Now, can we go to the DIY store? I want to look at some hammers."

Reader, I looked at hammers.

My, my. A hammer.

And what is this? Another hammer perchance?

Is this ... let me guess ... another hammer similar in almost every way to all its fellows?

How can I bear so much excitement without bursting?

To avoid dying of boredom, I started wandering around the shop. I spotted Valerie peering at us over a shelf.

She did NOT take the ceiling glue. Terrible liar – if you tell a lie, you have to commit to it. Obviously I'm not telling lies any more, but I still take a professional interest in the lies of others.

In the evening, Hyrrokkin made me feed her snakes – the ones she usually uses as reins for her wolf. But since the wolf is currently in dog form, the snakes are getting a rest. She's keeping them in a glass case, which is apparently a human custom.

Delightfully, I got to feed the snakes a live mouse  or two. I think they were grateful. The snakes, obviously. The mice were less than pleased with the whole situation.

Heimdall spent the evening reading about a mortal war that happened since we last came to Earth. The book made him very angry.

They use things called BOMBS now! Cowards! You should look into your enemy's eyes as you slay them. I don't know. Kids these days. No one knows how to hack off a limb!

Hyrrokkin suggested that since the book made him angry he should read something else, so he switched to one of his parenting books. This was bad news for me, because the book said that children should do chores to learn discipline. What does *this* book say chores are?

Chores: pointless, thankless tasks that need redoing on a regular basis, such as cooking and cleaning. The very definition of futility.

We never did chores as gods because Asgard cleans itself and food magically appears on our tables every time we have a feast. Which is every day.

So now my chore is the washing-up, which means scrubbing greasy plates and squirting them with a pungent green liquid.

Thor doesn't have to do chores because he's not here for moral improvement. It's so unfair! Also, Heimdall warned me to wear special gloves while I did the washing up. I will not do what I am told, so I did not wear the gloves. Now my hands resemble shrunken, shrivelled prunes. **THE INDIGNITY!**

Day Twelve:
Sunday

> **LOKI VIRTUE SCORE OR LVS:**
>
> # -3500
>
> **For making several mortals cry after stinging internet insults, including a number of adults.**

Over breakfast the next morning, I told Thor of my conversation with Valerie the day before. He agreed that she was PERHAPS following us, although he'd clearly been too absorbed by the hammers to notice at the time. Dullard.

"Maybe the Frost Giants have sent a spy to follow me," he said.

"Oh, of course, it's ALWAYS the Frost Giants," I scoffed. "And it's ALWAYS about you, isn't it?"

GRRR

"Look, Loki," he said, not bothering to swallow and showing me the mushed-up breakfast cereal in his mouth. "You can mock all you like. But they are my sworn enemies, and it would make sense that they would plan an attack when I'm at my most vulnerable, in a mortal body."

Thor is so obsessed with Frost Giants that it's his answer to everything ... but even someone with only one answer can be right from time to time.

Luckily, I had the perfect way to test whether this was one of those times.

I wrote down a statement in the book.

VALERIE IS A FROST GIANT SPY! FACT!

I waited for a second. Then...

> **Correction: Valerie is NOT a Frost Giant spy. She is a human girl. And this book is not intended to be your own personal soothsayer. You can have that one, but next time you try to test whether something's true using the book, Odin will be alerted so that he can come down there himself to "discuss" it with you. He'll be bringing the snakes.**

Hmm... This is annoying actually. I wasted my one chance to use the book to check the right answer to something, just when I have a Maths test tomorrow!

Day Thirteen:
Monday

School. AGAIN. How do children do this for so many years? Every day drags like when the god Balder does his performance poetry at a feast. You're trapped in a series of rooms, made to stay in one spot, forced to obey instructions. It's like being in an army, except you don't even get to fight anyone. All the downsides, none of the fun stuff.

SILENCE, HORRIBLE MAGGOTS!

I mean, I've never technically been in an army. But I've watched Thor fight a lot of battles while I shouted encouraging insults from the sidelines.

There's no fun and no shouting in school – well, no shouting from me, that is. The teachers shout freely and often. Usually AT me. Even though I got all the right answers in my Maths test!

(OK, so I copied all those answers off Valerie, who was sitting in front of me. But it's not my fault she doesn't cover her answers properly.)

I'm starting to get intensely annoyed about my quest. The more I try to be good, the more points I lose! I can't understand it.

However, into every life, some sunshine sparkles, even in dark times of bitterness and suffering and unfair points systems. Today, the sun beat down a full glorious blast upon me. For today was the day I discovered the greatest of mortal inventions: crisps.

These are sliced fried potatoes.

But they are so much *more* than that. They come in what appear to be millions of flavours, all created solely out of chemicals, so they do not contain the substance of which they taste. As a god of chaos and trickery, I applaud this deception. For example, there are bacon crisps that are vegetarian. They have never even touched a pig! True art!

I came to these glorious fried slices of Valhalla thanks to Valerie. She swapped me two packets for a carrot, so she could feed it to her horse. More fool her. Carrots are pathetic. Crisps are everything.

The moment I returned home, I would demand that Hyrrokkin and Heimdall buy large quantities of this glory food. Thor was very sceptical.

It was the first time in many years that Thor had been impressed by anything that I had shown him.

For a moment I wondered if it showed that, just maybe, one day we might become friends.

You know, you're not always completely wretched.

For Thor, that was a very positive thing to say about me.

"Huh!" I snorted. I didn't want to show him that I wanted to be friends. Weakness is something that others will always exploit. "I hardly think that a shared love of crisps is a foundation for true friendship, do you?" I said.

Thor looked a little hurt. I wonder why?

! I have some theories.

I was wondering out loud. I wasn't asking you.

! Fine, don't tap into my eternal wisdom.

Thor went over to talk to some boys and they fawned on him like abject peasants. While I waited for him to finish being worshipped, the school cat came over to be stroked. It rubbed against my legs and purred until I knelt down and stroked it. At least somebody appreciates me.

Day Fourteen:
Tuesday

LOKI VIRTUE SCORE OR LVS:

-3600

50 points lost for hurting Thor's feelings.

Hmm. I suppose that MIGHT be considered fair. But what need have I of Thor? For I – the great god Loki – made a new friend today.

Thor was kicking things with his sports-crazed friends, so I began talking to a boy from my class who was standing on the sidelines of the ball-kicking shenanigans.

I have been observing how humans have conversations, and it usually begins with talking about something you enjoy or something you hate. Since I find hate easier, I went with that.

This wasn't going as well as I had hoped.

At that point I gave up and walked away.

I walked and walked and walked alone until I saw a fox snuffling around at the edge of a park near a bin. Foxes are one of my favourite animals, so I followed the fox to its den, transforming into a fox myself so I could hang out with it for a while.

I came home late for curfew, and I'd ignored all Heimdall's text messages while I was in fox form. Heimdall made me write lines.

I AM SCUM AND DO NOT DESERVE TO LIVE IN ASGARD.

I AM SCUM AND DO NOT DESERVE TO LIVE IN ASGARD.

I pointed out that wasn't very kind of him. He said that HE wasn't the one who'd done such terrible things that he had to prove himself worthy.

Have I mentioned I hate Heimdall?

! Careful. It is unwise to insult one of the mighty gods of Asgard, who is not only beloved of Odin but also cooks your dinner most nights.

This is ridiculous. Hating Heimdall? He hates ME and no one minds! I quit. I can't do this stupid quest. Being good is too hard. Odin has set me an impossible challenge, just to watch me fail. How dare he? Who died and made him Allfather?

> **He did. He died and came back to life while on a quest for wisdom.** !

Look, I just don't care any more. This isn't working. I hate this. I HATE IT.

My fake parents hate me, Thor hates me, I don't understand how to talk to stupid humans and even the fox left me for an overflowing bin bag.

> **Technically, Thor doesn't hate you. He's just angry.** !

Shhh. Can't you see I'm having a self-pitying rant?

I'll never get back to Asgard according to THEIR rules. They never liked me, not from when I was a little baby giant (or half giant, no one's exactly sure). They were always mean to me. So, why should I be good to them?

If I AM as bad as they say, then I might as well give up trying to be good. What's the point?

So there. I quit. I'm going to find another way to Asgard – not as Odin's servant, but as his master.

I'm going to go back up there and take over. I don't care if writing this makes me lose even more points.

I QUIT!!

Day Fifteen:
Wednesday

Well, I have had a most interesting day. It all kicked off while I was in the toilet.

Oh, hello, I thought as something furry brushed past my bare legs.

It was the school cat again, purring and pushing her little cat face against me. *Wow, she must really love me*, I thought. *If she'll brave this place for me.*

The school toilets are smelly. I was only in there for the solitude and was holding my nose to make it bearable.

NO FINGERS AND THUMBS

CANNOT HOLD NOSE

On my way back to class, where I decided I would spend the lesson plotting to take over Asgard somehow, I bumped into Valerie. She gave me one of her odd looks.

After school, I went back to the toilets to see if I could find the cat that didn't exist. I did – but only for a moment.

When the cat saw me, it reared up on its hind paws and hissed. Its furry body shook and wobbled and grew, bigger and bigger, taking on a new shape...

It was a very tall, broad-shouldered woman wearing armour and carrying a mace. Her skin was very pale blue – with a layer of ice all over it, like a pane of glass in winter.

Greetings, Loki. I have a proposal...

The Frost Giant laid out her offer. "If you help me kidnap Thor, our sworn enemy, my king will lend you an army of giants to storm Asgard," she said. "You can go home in triumph. What do you say?"

I gulped. But I didn't hesitate for long.

"Deal," I said.

Day Sixteen:
Thursday

Shush, book!

Yesterday, the Frost Giant – let us call her General Glacier – explained her plan, as all good villains must. I, naturally, improved upon it. All that's required is for me to ensare Thor. Not exactly a challenge.

Sadly, I failed to take into account the fact that Thor has become what humans call "popular". This means all the other humans want to spend every waking moment with him. The boys on his sports team always want to play sports with him, or talk about sports. I'm not sure – I don't bother listening any more. They might be talking about milking sheep to make cheese for all I know.

SPORTS BALL!

Other manly things!

Sucks not to be us.

We are mighty and universally beloved.

The result is that it's hard to get Thor alone. But I shall bide my time like a patient spider, spinning my webs of lies and cunning. Also, I shall flick snotballs at Thor when he's not looking. The human body DOES have its advantages – it's a factory of disgusting substances, perfect for sly revenge.

I'M WAITING!!

Perfect for flicking

SNOT

FARTS

Easily disguised in yellow foodstuffs

EARWAX

Can be directed in an enemy's face and blamed on them

When Thor and I were shopping, I saw a woman working in a cafe spit in the coffee of a customer who was rude. I think I might be in love with her. Or I want to be her; I can't decide. I used to look down on mortals, but they've got spirit! And spit.

Have a nice day

After the original cluster of sportsboys left Thor alone, a bunch of adoring new fans surrounded him, asking him about his old school, which was apparently the most fascinating place on Earth, even though it doesn't exist.

The most galling part is that Thor is terrible at lying, so he started to run out of things to say about his last school, and I had to help him!

Stupid Thor's stupid handsome face.

Later that day, I bumped into Valerie in the corridor in between classes. I'd given up on trying to get Thor alone – it was too annoying watching all the people flocking around him. Valerie looked strange. Her face was swollen and puffy, and her eyes were wet.

She'd been crying.

Crying is one of the bodily functions gods share with humans, and one I do a lot of, without shame.

The usual Asgardian response to tears is to yell at you and call you a weakling. I suspected that wouldn't work on Valerie. She might punch me.

"What happened?" I asked her.

She looked at me, full of distrust. I'm very used to that sort of expression.

"Nothing," she mumbled.

As a lord of lies, I knew a lie when I heard one. But it wasn't my problem, after all, so I let her go on her way. Being a better person is no longer my job. All I need to do is trap Thor, and Asgard will be mine!

You'd think I'd feel a bit more cheerful about it.

I should feel like this.

Why do I feel like this?

Day Seventeen:
Friday

LOKI VIRTUE SCORE OR LVS:

**Honestly, it's better
not to think about it.**

Blah blah feelings.

The school day went by as slowly as a river of treacle. First, we had assembly.

How does that feel?

PINCH!

I spent the next five minutes enduring something mortals call a "dead leg". Thor needs to learn to use his words, not his fists, like our teacher said.

RIP

DEAD

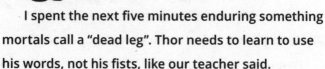

Didn't matter though. My plan was in place. The trap was set. Thor's time of punishment would come… I just had to survive the rest of the school day.

When that eternity of tedium ended, I sidled up to Thor as he was striding down the corridor towards the sports field. It was football practice after school. I was to watch while he kicked a ball up and down some grass.

It's nice that you like football so much.

UG.

I went on. "Thing is, I wonder if you're going a bit … human. There's no real danger in football. Though now that you have a mortal body, it makes sense that you'd do something nice and safe."

Thor stopped. "Are you trying to say I'm a coward?"

"Oh no!" I gave him a horrified look. "Of course not! You're just being sensible."

Thor gave me one of his thunderous looks, followed by some actual thunder rolling overhead.

"That wasn't me," said Thor, lying very badly.

"Still," I said as Thor began to walk again – more slowly this time – towards the sports field. "A less sensible person than you might look for something a bit more challenging. One of the younger kids told me that there is a giant alligator that is loose in the school, with teeth like razors and jaws the length of a car. They say it escaped from a zoo nearby and found its way into the school through the sewers. It would take a real hero to go and find it. But I realize you don't do that sort of thing any more. Very wise."

I'm imaginary.

Thor practically roared with fury.

"Where is this beast?" he growled.

"The little kids saw it crawling into the basement," I said. "I merely say that as a point of information. I wouldn't for a moment suggest going to find it. In fact, I would advise you VERY strongly not to."

"Hmm," said Thor. He thought about this, then his eyes lit up.

Aha! I see what you're doing!

I swallowed. For a moment, I thought he had seen through my reverse psychology. Maybe he was not quite as brainless as I'd always thought?

"You're trying to make me weak!" he finished. "Trying to stop me from doing what is right and brave! I should do exactly the opposite of what you tell me to do, Trickster!"

This is almost too easy. Like stealing babies from a mortal.

He stomped off towards the basement of the school, with me following. Every single one of his strides took me two trotting steps. Honestly, Odin could have given me a bigger body! It's not like he's short of power! Personally I think he found the idea of me trotting after Thor like a pony after a racehorse hilarious. RUDE.

Thor pulled open the door to the basement and we went down into the damp-smelling underworld beneath. Having scouted the space out, I knew what we would find.

DAMP

As Thor made his way to the farthest corner of the basement to find the alligator, he missed the whacking great giants creeping up on him down the basement stairs...

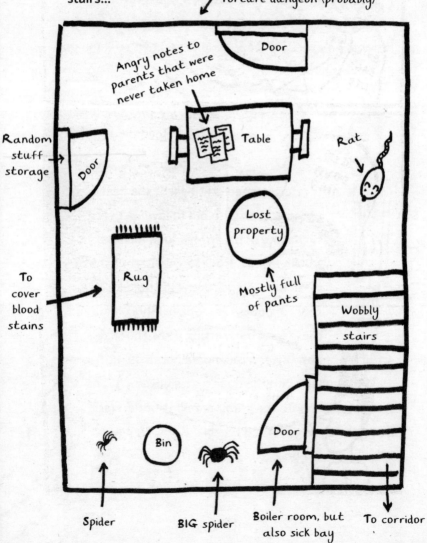

"I'm ready for my reward now," I said to General Glacier, the Frost Giant with whom I'd made my solemn pact. (Of course, I don't know if she was a general, but she did have a certain air of authority.)

She passed the Thor-bag to her companion, let's call him Captain Icebeard, for he was very beardy and extra frosty, even for a Frost Giant. General Glacier then reached for something from her pocket. Another bag...

It turned out that I was not the only person there who was in the betrayal business. I'd been double-crossed. ME!

But I wasn't beaten. I still had a few tricks up my sleeve. So, with a little Loki magic, I transformed myself...

I was free! I was free! I was...

Trapped. TURDS!

The two giants leered in through the glass at me as I buzzed helplessly. It occurred to me that as a mortal – whether human or fly – I would soon be running out of air in this little prison. But if I transformed where I was,

I might be cut to ribbons by the splintering glass as I grew to human size.

They say you always have a choice. But my current predicament only offered bad choices.

I considered a third bad choice: call for Odin's help. But, given that I had just betrayed his favourite son to the gods' sworn enemies, I suspected I'd probably get worse from Odin than I'd get from the giants. He might upgrade my eternal snake torture to something involving fire and needles.

"Let's discuss this," I said in my tiny fly voice. "Surely there's something I can offer you? Let's make a deal!"

The giants just laughed. But then...

I was free! I quickly flew out of the basement, followed by a wet and furious Thor.

We wouldn't have long before the giants regained their footing. But I was out in the corridor! PHEW! I changed back into my true form just as Thor came up the stairs behind me.

Moments later, Valerie Kerry appeared from behind a bookshelf, where she'd been lurking, holding some wet paper towels in her hand. I realized I was very pleased to see her. Not because I like her, you understand, but because she might provide me a very handy human shield to put in between myself and the furious Thor. But as Thor joined me at the top of the stairs, what she said next distracted him from his wrath.

"I knew it!" she said, her eyes gleaming. "I know what you are!"

Thor's jaw fell open. Even mine sagged slightly.

Had she seen me display my powers? No, surely not, for I changed before she could have seen. What then? How had she worked out our true divine nature?

Thor stared at Valerie. I stared at Valerie. Valerie stared at both of us.

"How about we discuss this somewhere more private?" I suggested, aware that angry Frost Giants might come up the basement stairs at any moment.

Valerie said she knew just the place.

As we walked after her, Thor hissed at me, "You've really done it now, Trickster. As soon as we've cleared things up with Valerie..."

GRRRR

He traced a finger across his throat in a gesture I did not like one little bit. It was definitely not a friendly gesture. Not unless you have the sort of friends who want to cut off your head.

We arrived at the promised destination, which turned out to be a sort of open prison for children, known as:

AFTER-SCHOOL CLUB

"I always end up sitting in the corner on my own and no one bothers me," Valerie explained as we sat on very squeaky plastic seats around a small table in the corner of a large classroom. A teacher stood guard in case anyone escaped.

"So," I said as casually as I could. "What makes you think we're aliens?"

Valerie's eyes flooded with a new light I'd not seen there before. Then she began to talk.

"So, I've always known there must be aliens out there. It only makes sense. The universe is infinitely large, and there are so many planets ... it's arrogant to think we're the only beings out there."

"True, true. Humans can be arrogant," I said. "But it seems you aren't. This is good."

"But ... we're humans too," said Thor, wrinkling his brow. He leaned in to me and whispered, not all that quietly, "Have you forgotten our cover story?"

I glared at him meaningfully and kicked him under the table. He kicked me back. It really hurt.

KICK

KICK

KICK

"It's too late," I said to him with a wink. You can't be very subtle with Thor, poor lamb. "She's rumbled us. She knows we're ALIENS," I said, hoping to Odin that Thor would gradually get it through his thick skull that it was a *good* thing she'd worked out we were unusual ... but jumped to the wrong conclusion. She'd never suspect we were gods now that she had an explanation for any oddness we might show her.

"Oh," said Thor. He looked very confused, but at least he stopped kicking me.

"When did you first suspect?" I asked her.

"The beginning!" she said. "I saw you arrive in your spaceship!"

This puzzled me. I definitely did not arrive in a spaceship.

Unless...

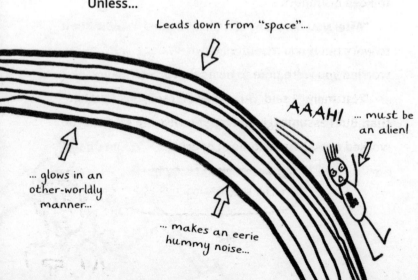

Leads down from "space"...

AAAH! ... must be an alien!

... glows in an other-worldly manner...

... makes an eerie hummy noise...

"Oh, yes, our rainbow-coloured spaceship," I said.

"Yes!" said Valerie. Her eyes glowed with excitement. "I mean, I say your spaceship, but I assume the main part of your spaceship is invisible, and that rainbow I saw was just the gangplank? Or some kind of tractor beam?"

Hi, I'm Loki.

"Its technical name is the Ritzymaplizzle, in our alien language," I improvised. It's the details that make a truly fine lie. "But yes, you might call it a gangplank or tractor beam in your tongue."

Thor was looking even more confused. I willed him to keep his mouth shut.

"After you arrived on Earth, I decided to follow you to work out if you meant us harm," Valerie went on. "I worried you were here to invade, you see."

"Naturally," I said. "An evil alien race might just do that. But I assume, given that you rescued us, that you worked out we have come in peace!"

But I like fighting, not peace.

143

I kicked Thor again, then quickly pulled my legs up under me so he couldn't return the favour. He finally got the hint and lapsed into sullen silence.

"Just my alien copilot's little joke. He comes in peace too. Do go on," I said to Valerie.

"I thought you might be evil invaders, but then Thomas stepped in to help me with the bullies. I still wasn't sure, though. It might have been a trick, to try to win my trust," she said. "But then I followed you into the basement just now, and I saw Thomas had been captured by aliens. And, using logic – which is a very important tool if you want to find out the truth, like I do – I worked out that you MUST be the good aliens, and they're the evil aliens, because they're doing the capturing! So I had to rescue you!"

"Bravo!" I said, giving her a clap. "Impressive deductive reasoning!" Mortal egos are fragile, and it is sensible to feed them.

Valerie just looked at me like I was weird. I decided to change the subject.

"How did you make the flood?" I asked.

"I blocked the toilets with toilet paper," said Valerie. "The plumbing in this school is really old, so it doesn't take much to cause a really big flood."

I made a mental note of that.

"Now," she said, pulling out a notebook. "I want to know EVERYTHING about life on your planet and who those evil aliens are."

I cracked my knuckles and grinned.

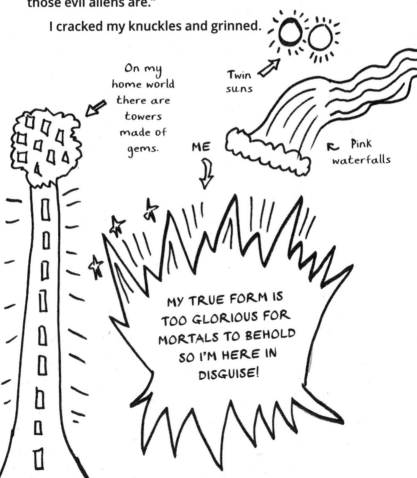

On my home world there are towers made of gems.

Twin suns

Pink waterfalls

ME

MY TRUE FORM IS TOO GLORIOUS FOR MORTALS TO BEHOLD SO I'M HERE IN DISGUISE!

"Why did you choose THAT body, then?" asked Valerie.

Thor snorted.

After I stopped smarting, I replied truthfully. "I didn't. It was chosen by my leader."

Another secret to top-flight lies: sprinkle just enough of the truth in with them.

Valerie took lots and lots of notes – and asked many follow-up questions, which I naturally always had answers to. In fact, she grilled me on alien life until the teacher came over and looked at his watch, asking if perhaps we wanted to go home soon? When I told him we were in no hurry, he retreated with a growl. HA! I saw through his ruse. Why do adult humans pretend they're asking if YOU want to do something when they mean THEY want to do it?

Valerie continued her questioning while Thor sat in sullen silence.

Our friendship might have been based on a web of lies, but I was really starting to enjoy Valerie's company.

She was very interested in me. Which is a prerequisite of any Loki-based friendship.

And hasn't my entire life always been based on a web of lies? Webs of lies are my comfort zone.

Mmm, comfy.

Thunderclouds formed overhead on my walk home with Thor. It began to rain, but only on me.

"You betrayed me to the giants," Thor snarled. Lightning flashed in his eyes. "You know what this means?"

"That you're easily fooled?" I said, wiping the rain from my face.

"That there's no way you're going to get enough points back by the end of the month to avoid eternal punishment," said Thor.

Oh. I'd rather forgotten all that in the thrill of telling Valerie about my life on an alien planet.

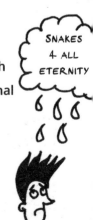

SNAKES
4 ALL
ETERNITY

No Frost Giant army for me.

Turds.

"And in our remaining time on Earth, I'm not going to even try to help you," Thor went on. "You're on your own. Unless you do something that threatens humanity, in which case, I'm going to squash you like the bug you are. In the meantime, I'm going to devote myself to guarding Earth in case those Frost Giants come back ... and I was RIGHT. I told you it was Frost Giants and you mocked me! But I was the one who was RIGHT!"

I hate it when he's right almost as much as I hate it when he farts on my head.

Note to self: fashion some kind of helmet to protect from Thor farts.

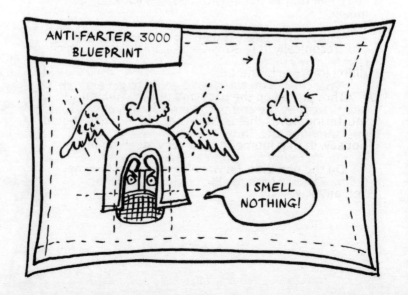

"Hmm," I said. "But it was I who pointed to the school cat when we first saw it and said it was a Frost Giant."

So, technically, I was right.

Technically, I could end your miserable life with one bolt of lightning,

He had a point, so I arranged my face into a pleading expression.

"You won't tell Hyrrokkin and Heimdall, will you?" I asked. For after all, he held my fate in his meaty, farty hands.

"No," said Thor. "But only because I'm not going to tell them that I – the mighty Thor – fell into a giant's trap."

"Technically, it was my trap," I pointed out, which didn't improve his mood.

Thor picked up the pace and left me behind, muttering words that eleven-year-old humans should not say. In that moment, I felt very much on my own.

On the plus side, he wasn't going to tell on me. Yet, anyway.

Problem

You're in BIG TROUBLE, Loki.

Day Eighteen:
Saturday

LOKI VIRTUE SCORE OR LVS:

Do you even want to think about it, Loki? Better to stick your fingers in your ears and sing la la la. For your doom is almost certainly eternal now. But I might as well tell you the full horror. You are currently at ... drumroll ... MINUS ONE MILLION POINTS!

OH. This is not good. Not good at all.

Problem

How WILL I ever get enough points to cancel out what happened with the giants? Even though I've managed to avoid showing my true godly powers to Valerie, that probably wouldn't count as a virtuous act, just the absence of a heinous error.

Problem

I decided to try a human tactic called "ignoring your problems and hoping they go away". I had observed it in many of the humans I met and thought it was worth a shot. So I searched the internet to discover what activities might be available to me to distract from my horrific reality.

I discovered a phenomenon called video games.

BIG problem

Games, Video: moving images controlled by mortal "players" that are often a form of simulated combat against monsters or armies, although others involve collecting magical items, as though you are on a quest. Others involve solving fiendish, brightly coloured puzzles. Mortal adults often mistakenly believe these games are responsible for all the ills of society, when in fact those ills are created by mortal adults.

At first, I scoffed at the idea of playing these games. Why *pretend* to kill monsters when you could just kill monsters? Or rather, sit back and watch Thor kill monsters from a safe distance, with snacks.

Then I remembered that I am stuck in the mortal realm where there are no monsters (except the ones at school), and Thor's hammer, which he uses to kill monsters while I watch, is on display in his bedroom gathering dust. So I thought I would give it a go.

I played one of these games on Heimdall's computer while he slept after his night shift and Hyrrokkin sampled a mortal pastime called gardening, which involved taking plants out of soil and putting them in different soil. I can't say I saw the appeal.

However, I *could* see the appeal of video games, which, it turns out, are BETTER than real violence. In real battle, you often can't hear yourself speak, so your enemy often mishears your pithy insults.

Not so in video games. Here you pit yourself against virtual foes all over the world via the internet and you can type insulting one-liners as you destroy them – and they can understand every word!

Sometimes, the insults hit home so well that you get a message back saying:

THIS IS GORGON0292's MOM. PLEASE STOP CYBERBULLYING MY SON. HE IS CRYING.

I think this means I won?

Day Nineteen:
Sunday

La la la la I'm not listening. Go away, problems, swiftly.

On the plus side, I got a new high score on my
violent game. I was merrily insulting my fellow players
when I heard a faint sound inside my mind...

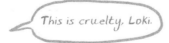

Wonder what THAT was about?

Day Twenty:
Monday

At breakfast, Hyrrokkin said I was looking very pale.

You should get outside more. Fresh air is good for mortals.

"But the air here is full of fumes," I pointed out.

She considered this. "Perhaps we should go for another country walk before school? Heimdall and I weren't around much this weekend. I understand that when mortal parents do this, they overcompensate with extra shared activities with their young."

"I'm going for a walk with the dog RIGHT NOW," I said before she could kidnap me for another torturous mudfest.

Thor came with me to make sure I didn't do anything terrible and to keep an eye out for Frost Giants. I tried to make conversation, but every time I said something, he merely glared. So I had to be alone with my own thoughts. That is usually a wonderful thing, as my thoughts are full of wisdom and insight.

Correction: your thoughts are usually full of trickery and insults. !

Hmm. Well. Anyway. Today my thoughts were full of none of those things. They were full of DOOM.

The only thing that broke up my gloom was the dog defecating. Even waving the poo bag in Thor's face didn't bring me my usual joy.

On the walk to school, Thor kept up his watch for Frost Giants and came very close to attacking a perfectly innocent cat.

At break time, Thor was inspecting every pupil he did not recognize in case they were a Frost Giant.

They made it easy by clustering around him.

Meanwhile, I made friends with some boys who had found a dead frog in the playground. This was distracting for a few minutes, until I suggested we should dissect the frog to see what's inside and they all backed away.

Valerie Kerry was made of stronger stuff.

A shadow appeared across our joy. I turned around to see... Fierce Boy One and his cronies!

This annoyed me greatly! It was NOT a good one. What kind of an insult is "frog girl"? I could come up with a better insult in my sleep! I stood up to my full, albeit limited, height and put my hands on my hips.

"Listen," I said. "I know you think that this pathetic display makes you seem manly and important, but have you ever considered getting a hobby, rather than bothering people with your inane nonsense? I hear sports are popular. Or perhaps you'd rather try your hand at crochet?"

"Huh?" he said. He clearly had the intellect of a Thor.

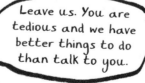

157

"Let's go," said Valerie. "It's time for class anyway." She threaded her arm through mine and we walked away.

"Thank you," she said. "It's honestly not necessary, but I'm glad to know you are such a noble alien, standing up against evil!" She looked pleased. At least, I think that's what her expression showed. It's not one I've seen before directed at me.

EYES NOT GLOWERING

LACK OF FROWN

STRANGELY UPTURNED MOUTH

"My pleasure," I said, and it was not a lie.

What WAS this warm, fuzzy feeling in my chest? Was I ... enjoying helping people?

Surely not. I am Loki. I am chaos. I am NOT a helper. I am, however, very good at insulting people. It's actually a tradition of the gods – the flyting: an insulting battle of words.

That warm, fuzzy feeling must have been pride. I was proud to bring a noble tradition of the gods to this poor excuse for a realm.

In this case, it really was not a fair fight. I picked my opponent to pieces in words, and he just said "huh" several times. I need better foes!

Speaking of foes, after school Thor met me at the gates. He'd avoided me all day but said he wanted to walk me home to prevent me from doing something terrible, like stealing a car or causing a plague or whatever.

Personally, I think he just wanted to get away from his fans for a while. Some of the boys were so clingy, it was embarrassing.

I definitely wasn't jealous.

Lie detected.　　　!

OK, maybe a little. Still... I had a friend of my own now. Odd.

Day Twenty-One:
Tuesday

> ## LOKI VIRTUE SCORE OR LVS:
>
> **Plus 1000** points for showing kindness and solidarity. So, minus one million to the power of infinity plus 1000, that's... Oh. Still not great, is it?

It seems I did gain a few points for standing up for Valerie, but it was merely a drop in the ocean. I have no idea how I'm going to gain enough now.

In Maths, Valerie passed me a note:

THANKS FOR YESTERDAY. YOURS IS A KIND PLANET. My phone number is on the back. Text me if you ever need help. Or if you have any good jokes.

Thor took it from me, suspiciously, after I'd read it.

"You ... did something kind?" he said with great confusion on his face. Much like the face he makes

when he has to work out how many fingers he's hacked off a giant.

"Yes, I did," I said, taking the note back.

"But you're a monster. You betrayed me to the Frost Giants! How can YOU do something kind?"

"I'm a complicated person," I said.

He just glared at me. "Still, I will never forgive you for betraying me," he said.

"Never is a long time," I said.

"So is Maths," said Thor, looking at the clock.

I laughed. It's unlike Thor to make a joke.

Then I felt an odd sensation. It was the opposite of the fuzzy feeling I had when I helped Valerie. It was bitter and prickly, like snake venom and cold steel in my chest. I couldn't put my finger on it.

In between classes, I asked Valerie, "What's that feeling you get when you've done something to someone, and it was … not good … and they say they won't forgive you and it's like you've swallowed rat poison?"

"Guilt?" said Valerie.

So... I feel guilty for betraying Thor, do I? That seems unlikely. I don't feel guilty for what I do! I am the trickster god. I skip over the surface of the world without even getting my toes wet! I don't feel GUILT for things. I do things and I move on!

The more I think about it, the more I think it was probably indigestion. Something with which my mortal body is now familiar after performing the human ritual of TAKEAWAY. (Very occasionally, Heimdall has good ideas.)

Takeaway: as humans do not have magical sources of food, sometimes they become weary of making their own sustenance and are even too weary to go to places called restaurants. In those cases, humans perform the ritual of takeaway, in which plastic containers of food appear steaming hot, commanded into being via smartphone.

This is my new favourite human custom. It is delicious!

Hyrrokkin did not approve, however. Apparently the plastic is wasteful and bad for the physical aspect of the mortal realm, and the food is corrosive to the internal organs due to things called "additives". Heimdall said it didn't matter about our internal organs, as we'd only be in these bodies for ten more days.

That killed my mood, as I realized I only had ten days left to prove I was worthy of Asgard rather than snake torture.

Planet Killers.

TEN...NINE...EIGHT...SEVEN...SIX...FIVE...FOUR...THREE...TWO...ONE...MEEEEEEEEEEE

Day Twenty-Two:
Wednesday

This morning, Heimdall and Hyrrokkin demanded to see the book to check on my progress. That would have been a very bad idea, I thought, considering I haven't made any. I've made the opposite of progress.

ME!!   PROGRESS

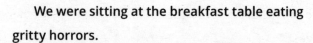

We were sitting at the breakfast table eating gritty horrors.

"Hand it over, Loki," said Heimdall.

"It's upstairs," I said. "Can I finish my unpleasant breakfast first?"

"Very well," said Heimdall.

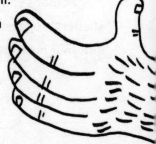

164

When Heimdall asked about the book, an odd expression passed over Thor's face.

"Well, OK isn't great, is it?" said Heimdall. "You'll have to try harder. I will see what my parenting books suggest."

"Perhaps you could volunteer at the local animal shelter?" suggested Hyrrokkin. "Watch out for ferrets. Bite your nose off, if you let them."

"Sure. Love ferrets," I said, not really listening. I was trying to work out what Thor was up to.

When we walked to school, I decided to come out and ask him. Subtle approaches were rarely any use with Thor.

"Why did you protect me?" I asked.

Thor grunted. Thor has many types of grunts. This was, to my surprise, the one at the bottom:

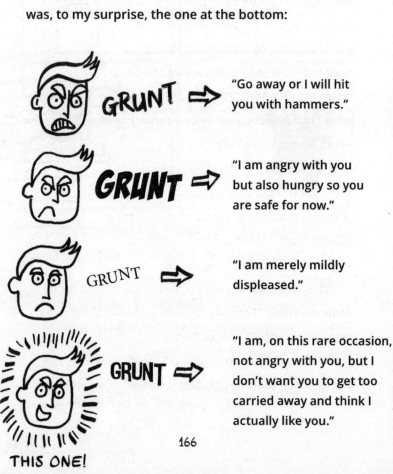

GRUNT ➡ "Go away or I will hit you with hammers."

GRUNT ➡ "I am angry with you but also hungry so you are safe for now."

GRUNT ➡ "I am merely mildly displeased."

GRUNT ➡ "I am, on this rare occasion, not angry with you, but I don't want you to get too carried away and think I actually like you."

THIS ONE!

"I didn't think you deserved to go to the snake pit. Not after being kind to Valerie," he explained. "It showed me there's hope for you yet."

Even though I betrayed you to the giants?

Thor shrugged. "That's just you being you ... but maybe you can be someone else. Someone better. I thought you should get another chance."

This gave me a lot of confusing feelings. I decided to squash them deep down inside and started up a conversation with Thor about which of two famous Frost Giants would win in a fight.

But after a short and animated discussion, Thor started to look worried. "I haven't seen any signs of those Frost Giants since..." He gave me a pointed look that said: *you betrayed me.*

Mockery

Witty insights

Poo jokes

The hidden things I do not admit to myself

The geology of my thoughts

This was a slight worry. Frost Giants didn't tend to be quitters. "Perhaps they've gone back home for reinforcements?" I suggested.

That was an even bigger worry. If there was one thing worse than two giants, it was an army of giants.

1 giant = Oh no!

2 giants = Oh nooooo!

Giant army = Oh noooooo...

PFFT

"I shall be ever vigilant!" said Thor. He looked at me distrustfully. "Hmmm, how can I be sure YOU are not a Frost Giant in disguise?"

"You can't," I said. "You better assume I am and be nicer to me in case I attack."

In response to that, he pushed me over onto the pavement and farted on me. I began to regret my playful words. Or at least my nostrils regretted them.

But as bad as Thor's farts are – and they are very upsetting indeed – they were nowhere near as bad as my points situation. I did a few sums and discovered that if I gained the same amount of points each day that I gained on my very best scoring day, it would still take me approximately nine squillion years, give or take an aeon, to show improvement overall and avoid the snake pit of doom.

(It wasn't terribly accurate Maths. But I was too sad for Maths.)

I AM DOOM!

168

I needed to take decisive action. I needed a big win! A good deed so enormous that it would cancel out that little matter with the giants and Thor.

My salvation came from a highly unlikely place: assembly.

Usually, we just get teachers talking at us, but today, we had a very handsome man in a well-cut suit. It turned out he was a local businessman. Surprisingly, he wasn't there to teach us how to be as wealthy and successful as him, so at first I was disappointed.

Instead, he gave a talk on the importance of charity. How it feels good to give back to the community and do something for someone other than yourself.

"Nothing you can buy feels as good as doing some good," he said.

I sat suddenly bolt upright. I'd had an idea. Something that would bring up my points total enormously...

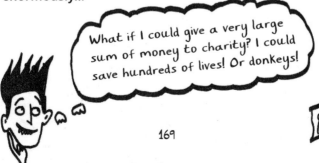

What if I could give a very large sum of money to charity? I could save hundreds of lives! Or donkeys!

I approached Fierce Boy One in the playground at breaktime.

"I hear you are very rich. I am very clever. Perhaps I could offer to do a large portion of your homework in return for cash?"

He threw back his head and laughed. "Sure, weirdo, you can do my homework, and I'll promise not to beat you up." He stopped laughing, apparently having an idea of his own. "There's something else you can do for me, though, and I WILL pay ... like ... a lot of money, if you do it."

I want you to make Valerie do something really embarrassing in public. Girls should be pretty and not weird. I want everyone to laugh at her. You figure out the details.

What he was proposing was, indeed, a doddle for the great god Loki. Embarrassing people in public is a particular speciality of mine – in fact, it's the thing that got me sent here in the first place.

OMG THIS IS SO EMBARRASSING! LOKIIII!

> All I have to do is find out what embarrasses Valerie.

For Sif, it was her vanity. For Valerie ... well, it's definitely not that. But I'll figure it out before too long. For I am Loki, the most cunning, the cleverest, the most about-to-make-a-lot-of-money-for-charity-est.

"Deal," I said.

"Nice one," snickered Fierce Boy One. "Can't wait."

In the class after that, I watched Valerie, wondering what she might be most embarrassed by. Then this incredibly annoying voice popped into my head. It seemed to come from the same part of me that that prickly, painful guilty feeling came from.

> Are you sure you want to do this? Embarrass her? Isn't that a BAD thing to do?

I shook my head. *No*, I thought back. *It's only a joke. She'll get over it.* The thing is, I'm going to be able to give SO much money to charity, it's going to give me a bazillion points.

The voice fell silent, but I could tell it was still in there, judging me.

171

I was also quite worried that I was starting to lose my mind. I went on the computer and searched:

I AM HEARING A VOICE IN MY HEAD TELLING ME NOT TO DO SOMETHING BAD.

Which is how I learned that the voice I was hearing wasn't a hallucination. It truly is my conscience. That's new.

Anyway, I think it was giving me bad advice. Surely doing something big and flashy that saves maybe hundreds of lives is the most important thing here? Who cares about tiny acts of kindness when there's BIG good to be done?

> Loki, I think you know the answer to that. If only you'd listen!

I don't think I like this voice. I'm going to ignore it. Conscience, go away. I'm not listening. If you try to talk, I'll put my fingers in my ears.

The amount of money I'll be able to give to charity is SO LARGE it should almost certainly outweigh any minor naughtiness, *and* all my previous misdeeds.

> THIS IS A BAD IDEA.

Sorry, what was that? Can't hear you. La la la la la can't hear you.

In conclusion, this is an excellent plan and the best way to free me from an eternal future of snake poison. And Valerie's just one mortal, after all. Even if she is my only friend.

But she'll forgive me. I'm so charming, right?

This seems unlikely.　!

How do I turn off comments on this thing? Hmm. Might just scribble them out...

That's better.

Crossing out words won't make them any less true.　!

Also, this does not seem likely to end well. As I believe your conscience is also trying to tell you.　!

Objection noted. Objection overruled. If my conscience is so clever, it should learn to speak up – I can't hear it over me singing.

la la la la

No, I am certain of this plan. This is going to be great. This is going to save me!

> **! I beg to differ.**

Has anyone ever told you you're really annoying?

> **! I'm a disembodied voice embedded in an enchanted book. No one tells me anything much.**

I'm going to bed!

Day Twenty-Three:
Thursday

I spent every moment I could with Valerie, trying to work out what she might be embarrassed by. There were lots of things other people found embarrassing that she didn't care about. Wearing mismatched clothes, for example, or farting publicly. (She and Thor had a farting contest in the playground today.) What DOES embarrass her?

Perhaps shaving her head?

She looks awesome!

Back to the drawing board.

She seems to be a little bit embarrassed by people paying her too much attention, but only a little. I think for Fierce Boy One to give me the money, it's going to have to be bigger than that.

> Humiliating someone is bad. You'll hurt her feelings.

I didn't know how to respond to my conscience, but then I read a bit of a book about being good from the library and it talked about how sacrifice – giving something up or losing something or going through something unpleasant – is part of being good.

So ... if Valerie has to go through something unpleasant for a short time, well, surely she'll understand. It's a sacrifice for the greater good!

Well, my greater good anyway. Surely the greatest good there is?

Day Twenty-Four:
Friday

Nonsense, it's brilliant. Shut up, book! In Music class
today, we were singing rounds, which means one
person starts singing a song, then another starts
afterwards, and then another. Given the vocal quality
of some of my fellow pupils, it was nothing short of
torture.

SQUAWK

One voice was more torturous than the rest. It was Valerie's. If you can imagine the squawk of a parrot, mixed with the sound a person makes when they've been vomiting for hours and there's nothing left in their stomach but bile and yet they're still retching, with something like the honk of a dying goose, you're only part way there to the true awfulness of Valerie's voice.

That in itself was nothing. As the song came to an end, Valerie was the last to stop singing. The look on her face when she was singing alone in front of the class was exactly the look I knew Fierce Boy One was after. That, and the fact that she burst into tears and ran out of the room.

WAAAAKK

All I need to do now is work out how to make her sing in front of a large group of people.

In the evening, Heimdall had his parenting books out again.

VERY TOUGH LOVE: THE MANLY GUIDE TO RAISING MANLY BOYS

I don't understand what's so great about being manly. It seems both the gods of Asgard and the humans of Midgard share this strange obsession. Ridiculous! First being manly is just whatever you do as a man. Second, it's a stretch to call me male. (I was a female horse, remember? And there's plenty more where that story came from...)

To avoid being lectured by Heimdall about how I needed to change everything about myself to be a better person, I ran upstairs and pretended to be asleep. Really, I was playing on my phone. I have discovered that there are tiny video games inside my phone as well as on Heimdall's computer. Joy!

Yawn. Sleepy now. One more game? There are some zombies in my phone that still haven't been eaten by plants...

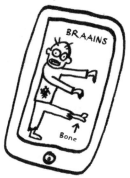

Day Twenty-Five:
Saturday

LOKI VIRTUE SCORE OR LVS:

Holding steady at: oh dear.

I slept late and woke to the sound of Thor and Heimdall doing battle. At least, that was what it seemed like by the sound of their fierce cries. In fact, they were shouting at a box in the corner of our meagre living room. The box was our new television, apparently. It's a machine that can show any story or exciting event in the world, but Thor and Heimdall chose to use it to watch mortals kicking a ball around some grass. I thought I was safe from sports inside my own home! But no. Apparently humans broadcast this dull torture to living rooms across the world!

It also seems that an important part of watching sport on television is shouting strange words at the television.

SSSSS   HSSS

In their state of nonsensical delirium, I could not reason with them. So I went to see what Hyrrokkin was doing. She was tending to her snakes, checking the temperature in their glass cage, while Fido slept at her feet, snoring.

"They are very beautiful, aren't they?" she said as the creatures slithered and hissed. "I think that when I return home I may not use them as reins any more, but set them free. I'll treat Fido to some new reins when he's a wolf again."

Snakes are beautiful creatures, it is true. But the eternity of snake torture in my immediate future has dampened my enthusiasm for them. I counted up my remaining days on Earth. Only six! After that, everything was going to sssssssssuck.

Apparently these thoughts made me look very grim, because Hyrrokkin took pity on me and took me out for a treat. Mortals like treats. This is because they do not have a daily feasting schedule, poor things. (And, lately, poor me.)

Hyrrokkin bought me ice cream, which I have to admit is almost as good a foodstuff as things you could get in Asgard. The Asgardian feasts are excellent, but they mostly consist of roast meats of various kinds with the odd honey cake. When I get back, I will have to introduce the gods to the concept of ice cream.

If I get back.

I still need to work out how to use Valerie's weakness against her in the most humiliating way possible. Then I'll win my way back to Asgard, and my future will be ice cream and joy forever!

Correction: it really, really won't. !

I can't believe my diary and my conscience are ganging up on me now. I won't listen to them. If I can't hear them, they can't hurt me.

Fine, ignore us. But it doesn't stop us being right.

What they said. !

I can't hear you. I'm asleep.

Day Twenty-Six:

Sunday

LOKI VIRTUE SCORE OR LVS:

I don't think you're even reading these, are you, Loki? Why do I bother?

My brai

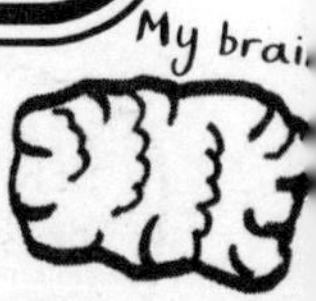

I asked Valerie if she wanted to do something together. As a cunning plotter, I decided that before asking her to do something for me, I should do something for her. This is clever psychology, because humans tend to think they owe you something if you do something for them. Manipulation and trickery are the only reasons I wanted to spend time with her. I do not crave the company or approval of mortals.

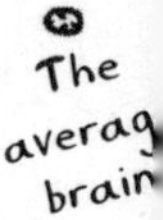

The
averag
brain

! A likely story.

Ahem. When she agreed, I was thrilled – at the success of my trick, OK? – and I said she should pick

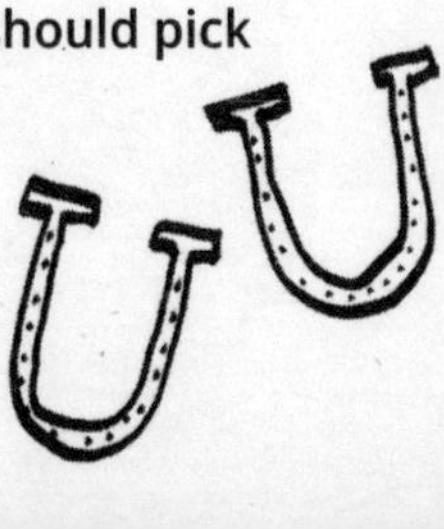

our activity. She picked going to see the horse she rides sometimes. The place we visited was near where Thor and I alighted from the rainbow bridge. The stables were not all that different from those thousands of years ago. While mortal technology has changed over time, the smell of horse excrement has not.

I happen to be quite good with horses – having been one once. Watching me pat the horse and seeing how it nuzzled into my hand made Valerie smile.

Lie detected.   !

Shush!

Day Twenty-Seven:
Monday

Today I found the answer to all my problems! So this diary knows NOTHING. Here's how it happened...

I was strolling down a school corridor in between lessons and, as I walked, I began to hum to myself. An old song from my real home, about crushing giants. A shout came from behind me.

I turned around to see the Music teacher. "Liam, you must enter my talent contest!" she said, coming at me with a leaflet as though it were a sharpened spear. "What a marvellous singing voice!"

Now, I had no desire to enter this foolish mortal contest. It would be too easy and not worthy of my skills.

But it gave me a genius idea.

"I'd love to," I said to the teacher, taking the paper and smiling to myself. "I have the perfect duet in mind..."

Sadly, my first attempt to persuade Valerie to enter the talent contest failed.

I needed a different, sneakier approach.

"It's a pity you don't want to enter the talent contest. I would very much like to take part in this important type of Earth-child culture, but I am scared to do it alone."

I tried to keep the trickster glint out of my eyes.

"Oh," she said, thinking deeply. "It *is* very important for you to experience all of Earth culture, so you can tell your people we are good and they shouldn't invade us."

"Yes, exactly," I said. "This will make invasion MUCH less likely."

"Then I will DO it!" said Valerie. "As long as you promise that we'll do it together?"

"On my honour as a citizen of the planet of Zarg," I said.

PLANET
ZARG
SALUTE

In the evening, Heimdall cornered me, waving his parenting book. "It says here that it's good for families to spend quality time together. I, as the man of the house, should present a strong male role model for my sons."

We're not a family. You're not my father. I'm not your son. I am only sometimes male.

"That's a mere technicality," said Heimdall. "Tonight we are going to spend quality time throwing a ball around in the yard."

189

"Sounds more like something you'd do to train a dog," I said.

Heimdall frowned and glanced down at his book. "Hmm... It says I should punish my sons for being cheeky."

I decided to try something.

"You're a poo-poo head," I said.

Why be a man when I can be anything?

Go to your room for the rest of the night!

What do you know? It worked! I was able to spend the entire evening playing computer games on my phone, with short breaks for videos of animals doing human things.

I'm a star!

Now that I'm sitting here, I realize something. My oath to Valerie that I would join her in song was sworn on a planet that does not exist. Therefore, I wasn't swearing a false oath. Odin would be proud!

190

Well, Odin would have nothing particular to complain about, then. Anyway. My plan is going to work, and I'm going to make so much money for charity that I'll win a million points, and then Odin WILL be proud. I'll go back to Asgard and everything will be good again.

> Loki, I think I'm losing you....

What's that you say? Maybe it will even be ... better than it was before? Perhaps Odin will be kinder to me? And Thor will be impressed with me? And everyone will carry me on their shoulders shouting "LO-KI, LO-KI, LO-KI!" And no one will act like I don't belong, and like I'm something they scraped off their shoe after taking Hyrrokkin's wolves for a walk?

LO-KI
LO-KI
LO-KI!

Day Twenty-Eight:
Tuesday

> ## LOKI VIRTUE SCORE OR LVS:
>
> 50 points lost for calling Heimdall a poo-poo head. As to the total, honestly, it's depressing even for me, a nonentity.

The talent show is tomorrow! Valerie is very nervous. I am not, naturally, because I don't get nervous. I am a god! I am Loki!

I do, however, have an upset stomach. Mortal bodies are silly.

Frequently fills with snot for the nose →

Objects to certain foods at random

I also have this strange feeling in my chest, like ants and spiders are inside me. Perhaps I have caught some human illness.

After all, I have nothing to be nervous about. Only Valerie does! Firstly, I love performing.

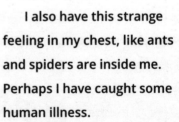

192

I often sing and perform poetry in the halls of Odin.

But, secondly, I'm not even going to perform!

In preparation for my grand plan, I started coughing in English class.

I assured her that I would be more than all right. (Actually, I will be the proud owner of millions and billions of points, thanks to my vast donation to charity.)

"I'll be right there with you, by your side," I said. Technically, this was true. I would be off to the side of her, and with her, in the sense of in the same room ... although not on the stage.

"I'm so nervous," she whispered.

This gave me another strange feeling. Not nerves. The guilt feeling. It also made that stupid conscience voice start talking more clearly again.

You shouldn't do this. You're going to hurt her feelings.

"Shhh," I hissed to the voice. "This is the plan. It's a good plan. It's the best plan."

After all, I am Loki. My plans are the most cunning plans in the world. I was sure, absolutely *sure*, that everything was going to be OK. Everything was going to be brilliant.

> **!** Unlikely. Everything would have a better chance of ending well if you set fire to your own head.

Overall, school was a source of dull despair. Although I am a god, I never understood the true meaning of eternity until I had to sit through a Science lesson. Why human teachers think it is a good idea to show eleven-year-olds how to create explosives, I cannot say.

The real shocker is that they manage to make explosives seem BORING. Bah.

> Instead of yelling FIRE IN THE HOLE, BOOM! I will now tell you a string of incomprehensible numbers that have something to do with the BOOM.

Valerie and I practised our song after school. I still can't feel the inside of my head after having Valerie bellow at me. But to achieve true virtue you must experience some pain, I suppose. And I have exoperienced A LOT, so I must be getting very virtuous.

I suggested we practice separately for a bit and sent her lots of encouraging text messages from a safe distance, at home.

Keep it up! You got this!

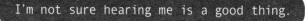
The neighbours just came round to complain.

They are philistines!

What's a philistine?

You know my brother Thomas? Like that. People who don't know a good thing when they hear it.

I'm not sure hearing me is a good thing.

Nonsense!

Then why are we practising at separate houses?

Because it's really important we both know our own parts.

That, dear reader, was a lie. Can I confess, afterwards, I felt a little bit sick inside? On the other hand, that might just have been Heimdall's cooking. He decided that I would show moral improvement if he's more nurturing towards me, so he is forcing me to eat his foul concoctions for every meal. Even when I said that eating crisps would make me much happier than this swill.

When Valerie texted to say how nervous she was, I got an even worse feeling in my stomach, and the voice spoke again.

> There's still time to change your mind. You know this will end badly.

I put on very loud music in my bedroom to drown out the conscience voice.

"Turn that down!" Heimdall yelled up the stairs.

Very hypocritical of him to tell me not to make noise when he was yelling!

Still, I turned it down. I couldn't risk making him too angry when I was so close to victory...

I went to sleep and dreamed I was a horse.

Day Twenty-Nine:
Wednesday

LOKI VIRTUE SCORE OR LVS:

Holding steady ... so far...

About my dream last night – I told you about the time
I was a horse? Remind me to tell you the part about
me giving birth to a foal with eight legs and giving it to
Odin as a present. True story!

NEIGH

> **!** **Reluctantly, I must confirm
> this is indeed a true story,
> however far-fetched it may
> sound.**

To Odin

Today is not the time for me
to tell you that tale in full, however. Everything has to
go perfectly, so I must focus.

Lessons were more irritating than usual. I found myself grinding my teeth, willing the time away. I wanted the evening to come. No, I didn't want it to come. I wanted it to have come AND gone. I wanted it to be over.

Not because I was dreading what I was going to do, of course. I was doing A Good Thing. I was saving babies! Or... I forget exactly what the charity I'm raising money for does. But probably saving babies. Or adults. Possibly endangered marmosets.

After one million years (approximately) lunchtime arrived. It was time for the talent show, and all the performers assembled backstage. Valerie and I were going on first. I felt oddly nervous. Valerie clearly was too. She was standing in a corner, biting her lip. I sidled up.

I felt the slightest flutter of something in my chest. Probably nerves, in case my genius plan didn't work.

"I can't do it on my own!" Valerie muttered.

"Go on, Valerie!" said a teacher. "Liam's poorly, so you get to do a solo! How exciting!"

It's incredible that teachers, who are supposed to know so much, often know so little.

She pushed Valerie into the middle of the stage, all alone. I pressed play on the musical accompaniment and Valerie began to sing. If you could call it that.

For the first verse of the song, the audience was completely silent. But then the titters of laughter began. The teachers were *shhh*ing everyone, but they could not stop it.

"What's that I hear?" called out Fierce Boy One. "Is someone killing a moose?"

"I don't know," said Fierce Boy Two. "But whatever it is, I think it's in pain!"

Onstage, Valerie began to tremble with shame.

I should have felt a rush of delight and glory. I'd kept my bargain. Instead, I felt oddly empty. The voice came again.

> Dude. I told you so. And, because I am you, deep down YOU told you so.

As she finished, Valerie ran offstage in tears.

I met Fierce Boy One in the locker room. He slapped me on the back.

Well done, mate. That was even funnier than I thought it was going to be.

He handed me a bag, containing more Earth money than I'd ever seen. It was genuinely almost too heavy for me to lift.

"Pleasure doing business with you!" he called after me as I left the locker room.

Outside, Valerie was waiting for me.

She looked down at the bag of money. Then she looked at Fierce Boy One, who was emerging from the locker room. He grinned evilly at Valerie.

Have you ever thought of going on one of those **TV** talent shows?

"Or … maybe a wildlife documentary would be more your speed?" He added before striding off, laughing to himself.

For the first time in my very, very, very long life, I couldn't think of a lie. All I could do was stare at her.

> I thought you were a good alien. But you're just... A HORRIBLE, SELFISH JERK!

"I'm sorry. I meant to do something good," I said. I felt my throat fill up with a lump of horror. She was getting it all wrong. She was getting ME all wrong. The point wasn't to hurt her. The point was to do something good!

"I'm giving all this money to charity, you see!"

> I'm a GOOD alien.

"Whatever planet you're from, you're a terrible friend," spat back Valerie. "Good luck with your life. I thought you could be a good person. But I was wrong. Goodbye," she said.

Valerie strode off, leaving me standing there with the bag of money. Thor arrived.

"What happened?" he asked. "Why didn't you perform with her?"

I sat down on the floor, feeling like all the air was gone from my lungs.

Thor glared down at me. "You tricked her, didn't you?"

I pointed at the bag of money. "It was all to make money for charity."

Thor exhaled and closed his eyes. "Oh, Loki. I really thought there was hope for you. But there's none." He shook his head. "I hope you enjoy your eternity of snakes."

I realized fully in that moment what had been dawning on me for the last half an hour.

I have made a terrible mistake.

You have made a terrible mistake.

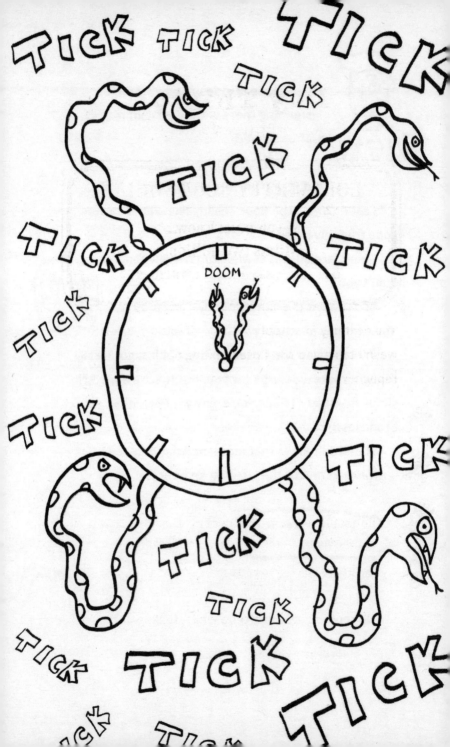

Day Thirty:
Thursday

> ### LOKI VIRTUE SCORE OR LVS:
>
> If you must know...
> Minus two million.
> But don't say I didn't warn you.

The next day at school was a fog of misery. Valerie wasn't talking to me. I tried texting her but got no reply.

 I'm sorry, Valerie. Forgive me?

 Valerie?

 Honestly, I'm really sorry.

 Valerie? Halloooooo?

No reply. I gave up after a while, feeling pathetic.

Who could have known the level of pain caused by a shiny screen that didn't even contain stabbing blades or poison?

The fact that my phone did not go *ping* to show a reply from Valerie made me feel sadder than the time I had my mouth stitched closed for losing a bet with some dwarves. (Long story, involving a ship you can put in your pocket, a magic hammer, and me only just escaping decapitation. I'll tell you about it when I'm less miserable.)

As well as Valerie ignoring me, the only thing Thor said to me was, "Tell me when you want me to call Odin to end it all."

Which was not, as you can imagine, very cheering.

My mind was scrambling, trying to think of ways I could somehow claw back my points. But honestly, I'd fallen so low, what could I do? Seeing the look on Valerie's face as we passed in the hall, I knew that I'd done something so awful to her, there wasn't any making up for it. Not even with a million pounds of charity money.

At least it would make someone else's life better, even if it wouldn't help me.

But I was lost.

Fierce Boy One accosted me at lunch, slapping me on the back. "Man, her FACE! I wish I'd taken a picture," he said.

"Do you?" I asked. My voice was laden with a millennium of weariness. Why did I think doing business with this jackanapes would ever lead me anywhere good? I thought I was being cunning. But it was the peak of stupidity. I had helped a cruel boy hurt someone.

Well done, Loki. Well done.

I walked away without even bothering to tear him into shreds verbally like the worthless waste of space he was.

Perhaps because I was beginning to sense that I was not exactly the GREATEST use of space on this Earth either.

After a particularly dull Art lesson, where we had to make works of art out of dried human foodstuffs, I tried to go over to Valerie and apologize properly. She ignored me and ran off down the corridor. I followed her at a distance and saw her sneak into the games closet where they keep all the footballs and other meaningless trifles.

I knew she wouldn't listen to me, so I looked left and right and checked that no one was looking. Then I transformed myself into a human girl, so she wouldn't know it was me and make me go away.

I could hear Valerie crying.

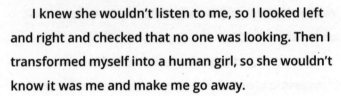

Her curiosity was starting to overtake her tears.

"I'm new. I'm..." I cast about for a suitable name, staring at the door of the cupboard. "Door. I mean, Dora. I heard someone crying and I thought I'd come and see if everything was OK."

"It's not really," said Valerie. When she came out of the cupboard her eyes were all red and her plaits had random bits of hair sticking out of them.

"What happened?" I asked.

"A boy happened. Several boys, in fact," said Valerie. We started to walk down the corridor. "Well, one of them is KIND of a boy anyway."

"He sounds interesting," I said. My heart was thumping a little bit faster.

"I hate him," said Valerie.

My heart seemed to skip over itself and fall flat on its face.

"I thought he was my friend, but then he did something horrible to me," Valerie went on.

"I'm sorry," I said.

Valerie shrugged. "Not your fault."

"Maybe he didn't mean it?" I suggested.

> Maybe he was trying to do the right thing but got confused about what that was.

"I don't think he'd know what the right thing was if it bit him on the bum," snapped Valerie. "He's just ... he's just selfish. He's not like the bullies here who enjoy being cruel to people."

> But his selfishness makes him cruel.

"That sounds ... bad," I said.

"Well, thanks for listening. It's nice to know not everyone in this school is awful. I better go to the next class."

I nodded and let her go.

Was that my imagination, or did I see that cat watching us?

Surely not. That's approaching Thor-level paranoia.

YOO-HOO!

Day Thirty-One:
Friday

So this was it. My last day on Earth. It felt especially cruel to spend it in school. Of course, Valerie would not talk to me. Fierce Boy One kept smirking at me as though we were friends. I wondered if, since I was probably damned anyway, I might as well do something horrifying to him before I left. But even the thought of that didn't cheer me up. In fact, the thought of doing another cruel act – even to someone who so clearly deserved it – made me feel dizzy rather than joyful.

Who even AM I any more?

213

The lessons blurred into one single smear of boredom and despair. I racked my brain to find something that might save me but came up with nothing.

After school I returned to discover that, horror of horrors, Heimdall had bought a new parenting book. As though that would save me.

THE LAST HOPE PARENT PLAN:

For desperate parents whose children are terrible even though they've tried everything

"It says in this book that families who do enjoyable leisure activities together are superior to families who do not," said Heimdall, tapping his book. "So tonight we are going bowling."

"What is bowling?" asked Thor.

"It involves throwing a ball at some sticks to make them fall over while wearing borrowed shoes," said Heimdall.

I thought that sounded stupid, but a tiny part of me was glad to do something all together. Being alone

with my thoughts was not something I was enjoying on this day. Usually my thoughts are the best and cleverest things in the world. But right now they were mostly:

EVERYTHING IS BAD AND SNAKES ARE YOUR FUTURE AND VALERIE HATES YOU.

The game itself was repetitive and tedious and, of course, Thor was PERFECT at it. He quickly turned the scoreboard into the Thorboard.

It felt a little too close to the bone, given my current points situation. Perhaps Odin was sending me a message through the scoreboard that he knew. Or perhaps I was just terrible at bowling, just as I was at being good.

POINTS TOTAL

Thor | Loki

100000 X 20 | HA HAHA NO.

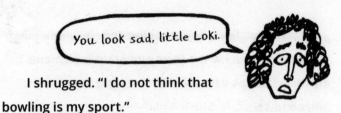

You look sad, little Loki.

I shrugged. "I do not think that bowling is my sport."

"Me either," said Hyrrokkin. "I prefer weight lifting and wolf racing."

"My favourite sport used to be playing tricks," I said. "But I'm losing the taste for it now."

"Well, that's good, isn't it?" said Hyrrokkin.

"I don't think it's enough," I said. "I suspect I'm going to fail Odin's challenge, and I'm going to be condemned to eternal punishment."

For some reason, Hyrrokkin's big serious face made me want to be honest for a change. I just started talking and couldn't stop, like word vomit.

"I think I've ruined everything," I spewed. "I've got no points, no friends, and no chance of making things OK again. So what's the point? I think I should just call Odin up now and tell him to end it."

I'm scared.

I didn't mean to say it.
It just popped out.

216

Hyrrokkin didn't say anything at first. Then she said, "When I was a young giant, in Jotunheim, I knew a giant a bit like you. She was a trickster who longed to be a god. She felt like everything was against her and that everything she wanted was out of reach. She was angry, and she lashed out and made enemies. One day, she had a chance to do something good. She knew it probably wouldn't change anything. But she did it anyway. I was out on the ice with my wolf – he was just a puppy then – and the ice began to crack. She saw me yelling for help and skipped over the ice and pulled me out just as I plunged into the freezing water. There was nothing in it for her, but she saved my life. And, more importantly, she saved my puppy."

I narrowed my eyes. "Are you going to tell me that was my mother, and I have it in me to do good, even when there's nothing in it for me?" I asked.

Hyrrokkin laughed. "How self-centred are YOU, little boy? Not everyone is related to you, nor is everything about you. There are thousands of giants who've never heard your name and are definitely not your mother. But it doesn't matter if your mother was a good person. You don't need to have good running through your veins to be good. You just need to do good." She gave me a pat on the shoulder that nearly knocked me over like one of the bowling sticks. Then she left me alone, listening to balls smashing against their target and feeling sorry for myself.

Then, I felt something vibrating on my leg. My phone!

They have me. I've been kidnapped. The evil aliens don't understand phones, apparently, so they didn't stop me from sending this. I still hate you btw. They said that I ruined their plans and they are going to take a terrible revenge on me. So come and save me if you are worth ANYTHING. Bring your spaceship or something. I'm at the school sports field.

PS I STILL HATE YOU.

BZZ

PPS If I die, please make sure my mums still go and fuss Rusty at the stables.

218

I rushed over to Thor.

Valerie's in trouble. The giants have come back!

I'm not falling for another of your tricks, Loki.

"But... Valerie!" I insisted.

"You're not going to persuade me you care about her after what you did," scoffed Thor. "Now go away. I'm bowling. Then I'm calling Odin so we can end this farce."

I was on my own. I slipped away from the bowling alley while the others were in the middle of a game. I ran all the way to the school and...

What were the giants going to do to Valerie? And what could I even do to save her? Thor was the strong one. I was the ... what? The sneaky one? The bad one? The betrays-his-friends one?

Valerie was in the centre of a circle of four giants on the playing field. I spotted General Glacier, Captain Icebeard, and two more slightly less impressive giants. Let's call them Corporal Coldnose and Sergeant McFreezy.

> Please don't eat me.

"There will be no eating," said General Glacier. "We will, however, take her hostage to lure the gods to us so we can bring them ALL to the dungeons of the king! Asgard will fall and we will be victorious for all eternity!"

I was in boy form, hiding behind a bush at the edge of the playing fields, and just then, a leaf tickled my nose...

AcHOO!

"Who goes there?" boomed one of the giants.

"Excellent," cackled one of the other giants. "We have him now too! But where's the handsome one?"

"Bowling," I said. I was too scared to even object

that the giant was calling Thor the handsome one.

"So, is that it?" asked Valerie. "You're captured, and these evil aliens are going to eat us?"

"Imprison you in our dungeons," corrected General Glacier. "We're not monsters."

"Look, I have something to tell you, Valerie," I said.

A plan was hatching in my mind, but it meant breaking the one absolute rule that Odin laid down. It was a one-way permanent ticket to Snakesville, no takebacks, no second chances.

I was going to have to show her my powers.

I had nothing left to lose – but I could win Valerie her freedom.

I'm not an alien. I'm a god. And they're giants.

Giants? They're not very big.

Then she peered at me. "And you don't look like a god. At all."

"And I don't often act like one either," I confessed. "But I want to for once. Now. Do you trust me?"

"I really don't," said Valerie. "You've just told me you've been lying to me this whole time, and you betrayed me, and—"

"OK, do you trust me more than those giants over there who've just said they're going to eat and/or imprison you in their dungeons?"

Valerie shrugged. "Maybe."

"Then here we go," I said, taking her hand. I let the magic flow through me, and her too, and transformed myself into a falcon. I turned her into a little nut and took her in my claws. Before the giants realized what I was doing, I launched into the air, with their cries beneath me.

You'll never catch me!

Aw nuts.

Valerie, in nut form, couldn't speak, but I felt her rattling, and I thought she might be trying to say "Don't taunt them until we're at a safe distance!"

The giants took on flying shapes of their own. One became an eagle. Another became a gigantic bat. It was pretty cool actually. They all launched into the air, chasing us. My wings flapped and I soared through the sky until I reached our destination, then plummeted down as fast as gravity could pull me.

Landing in the car park of the bowling alley, I transformed us into our human forms. We ran through the door to the bowling alley. Everyone inside the place turned to look at us.

Our foes swooped through the door behind us, still in bird form. Seeing the air full of terrifying shapes, all the human bowlers screamed and ran.

The flying beasts began to grow and change into their true shapes.

"**GIANTS!**" cried Thor, observant as ever. He hurled a bowling ball at them.

Hyrrokkin whistled, and her wolf-in-dog's-clothing came running. Who takes pets bowling?

Well, Hyrrokkin, clearly. The wolf shook off its doggy form and grew ... and grew...

Heimdall pulled out a mighty sword, which must have been stored somewhere uncomfortable.

They were a mighty sight to behold.

Gods in human form are still gods, after all.

GASP!

Then the fight began. It went something like this:

A short while later, the dust settled, and the giants were beaten.

"You win this time, Asgardians," said General Glacier, whose armour had a bite mark from Hyrrokkin's wolf.

GRRR

"But we will be back," said Captain Icebeard, whose beard was smeared with tomato ketchup from where Thor hit him with a dirty food tray.

"And we'll be ready," growled Thor.

"In fact, why don't we just settle this once and for all now?" suggested Hyrrokkin. She was brandishing a broken chair and looking even more terrifying than usual.

I can take you all.

The Frost Giants, battered and bruised, exchanged glances.

Then they ran away as fast as they could, shrinking to human form.

Did you see me punch that giant?

No. All I saw was you hiding under a table.

I had to admit, I HAD done less fighting than I'd done hiding.

"But thank you," said Valerie. "It wasn't a rubbish rescue."

To my surprise, she gave me a hug.

Heimdall and Hyrrokkin escorted all of us – including Valerie – back to the safety of our mortal abode.

We sat around the table drinking hot liquids. Valerie demanded to know everything.

"Since she's seen you use your powers, the damage is done, I suppose," said Hyrrokkin. "But you'll have to answer to Odin."

"What do you mean?" asked Valerie.

"Odin's one rule was that Loki must not reveal his powers to mortals. We have a treaty with the other gods, and to break it is eternal torture," said Heimdall.

You did that, for me?

I ... suppose so.

"Yes, you did," said Odin. He was all of a sudden at the table with us. My blood ran cold. The hot tea turned to poison in my mouth.

Not literally, I'm just being dramatic.

"I'm sorry, Allfather," I said. "I broke the one rule. But, in my defence..." I trailed off. I was tired. I was out of tricks. I was caught. "I don't have a defence. Take me to the snakes."

NO.

Odin fixed me with his solitary eye for what felt like an eternity.

Then he said something very surprising.

"I won't send you to your snakey punishment just yet, Loki. Although you have done many terrible things here on Earth, including breaking one of our most sacred rules... I truly believe you have changed. You've shown you can put someone else before yourself. That gives me hope that you could one day be worthy of Asgard."

I sat staring at him with my mouth open like Thor when he's eating.

Heimdall, Thor, Hyrrokkin and Valerie all exchanged looks.

"Look, I'm not going to pretend you're a good person yet," said Odin. "You broke the rules, but for the right reason – to protect your friend. You're changing. So perhaps I can change too. Even an old man like me can be a little flexible with the rules. What I propose is a new deal. Your new quest is to protect the mortals from Frost Giants," said Odin. "And from all other threats from all the other realms."

"So I don't have to write in that stupid diary any more?" I gasped. "I can be a hero instead?"

"I should clarify. Your new ADDITIONAL quest," said Odin. "You still have MUCH progress to make and must report back in the diary every day."

"Oh, OK," I grumbled.

"Now, you," said Odin, turning to Valerie. "You must swear you will not tell another mortal soul what you have learned."

"I swear I won't! On my horse!" said Valerie solemnly. "I can't believe you're not aliens though. What about—"

"Goodbye for now." Odin clicked his fingers and Valerie was gone.

Shame. I really wanted to tell her more about my fabulous true self! Still, things were looking up.

"So ... I'm really not going to be punished with dripping poison and snakes?" I asked.

"Not unless you do something else to deserve it," said Odin.

"And I ... stay here and protect the mortals?"

Odin nodded.

"Very well," said Thor. "Then I will stay with him."

Odin blinked his solitary eye. "What?"

"It is a worthy quest," said Thor. "And Loki needs my strength by his side."

"It's true, I do," I said, faking a punch in the air. "Arms like noodles."

"Then we will stay too," said Hyrrokkin. "I feel there is more to explore here on Earth. Plus, it turns out I like bowling, in spite of myself. The shoes are VERY comfortable. And I'm just starting to get a lot of followers on my social media. I post about my snakes a lot and it appears the people of Earth truly love snakes."

234

Heimdall shrugged. "Ah well. If everyone else is staying... I can't abandon my family."

"We're not a family," I said.

"Aren't you?" asked Odin. He chuckled. I hated his wise chuckles usually, but this one made me feel oddly warm, like when you urinate while swimming in a cold northern sea.

"Well, I better get back for tonight's feast," said Odin.

"Send my love to everyone," said Thor. "Even Aunt Freyja's cats."

"And send my…" I tailed off. The last time I'd seen everyone in Asgard, they'd been furious with me. "Erm, maybe don't mention me."

"I will tell them of your deeds on Earth," said Odin. He even smiled!

I found myself grinning back.

Then he disappeared in a flash and a bang and I was alone with my sort-of family. I didn't know what lay ahead, apart from – most likely – attacks from angry giants. I didn't know if Valerie was still my friend. I didn't know if I'd ever be worthy of Asgard. But I knew that, for once in my strange angry life, I was not alone.

"By the way," said Heimdall…

You are so very GROUNDED.

TO BE
CONTINUED...

Acknowledgements

KAREN LAWLER.... The Best Wife for
All Eternity

MOLLY KER HAWN... Agent of Asgard

NON PRATT... Word God

LINDSAY WARREN... Word God Over
the Water

JAMIE HAMMOND... Art God

KIRSTEN COZENS... She of the
Publicity Pantheon

KAREN COEMAN... Translated Being of
Pure Light

RACHEL FATUROTI... Norse God of No

MARK BRADLEY... Panel Border God

DAN BERRY... Comics Giant

TEAM SWAG... Emotional Support Horses

FEMINISM 2.0... Mortally Insightful Women

ALICE, HELENA AND VICKY... Mighty Valkyries

DAVID AND ROBIN... Dog-adjacent Deities

ABBIE AND ELIZABETH... Black Hole Norns